"I would have happily divorced Will."

After searching for a tissue, Isabel continued, "And told Faith I never wanted to see her again, but I didn't want them dead. Do you?"

"I'm not sure." He wasn't sure about anything. Faith had left a note before she'd driven away with Will. She'd claimed Will had turned to her for comfort because Isabel had rejected him. If not for Isabel, they'd never have grown close enough to fall in love.

Even if that was true, was their adultery really Isabel's fault? Shouldn't Will have fought for his marriage? Ben had known he and Faith had problems, but he'd never considered divorce.

Shutting Isabel's door, he walked along the side of the car. His best friend had made love with his wife and created the baby who slept in a crib down the hall.

And Isabel had known. With a few words, she could take his son for her family. He imagined himself in her place, watching her mother fall apart, her father walk around like a monolith without emotion. And Tony could make them both better.

How could he trust her? Until he knew what she was going to do, he couldn't let her out of his sight.

Dear Reader,

Right now, in my world, family is a fragile thing. Ironically, I've just finished a story with the same theme, *Another Woman's Son*.

The relationships in this novel are complex. Ben Jordan and Isabel Barker both knew they had problems in their marriages, but they had no idea they'd lost so much until all they had left was the small boy who binds them together. In the end, they discover that, along with the boy, they have a mutual talent to love and forgive and create a future.

As I wrote this book, I began to realize that loving and forgiving are the best gifts we can give our families, no matter how we grow or fracture or adapt. If a moment comes that requires everything we have to offer, love and forgiveness are good places to start.

I hope you'll enjoy this story that remains with me still. I'd love to hear from you. E-mail me at anna@annaadams.net.

Best wishes,

Anna Adams

ANOTHER WOMAN'S SON
Anna Adams

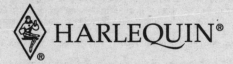

TORONTO • NEW YORK • LONDON
AMSTERDAM • PARIS • SYDNEY • HAMBURG
STOCKHOLM • ATHENS • TOKYO • MILAN • MADRID
PRAGUE • WARSAW • BUDAPEST • AUCKLAND

ISBN 0-373-71294-4

ANOTHER WOMAN'S SON

Copyright © 2005 by Anna Adams.

www.eHarlequin.com

Printed in U.S.A.

Books by Anna Adams

HARLEQUIN SUPERROMANCE

To the three I lost last week:

Edith Taylor Adams
I have many mothers, but you were the one who loved
me out of choice, from the day I met you. Thank you for
my husband and my "brothers," for the you in Sarah's hands
and Colin's smart mouth and Jen's ambition and Stevie's
willingness to always try something new. The plan still goes—if
this thing with Steve doesn't work out, you and I are always
Ma and daughter. I love you.

Aunt Daisy
You were the sophisticate in our family. You plucked your
eyebrows and indulged in a bit of the grape, and I hear your
smoky laughter right now. I loved your stories so much, the
anticipation was more than half the fun. In fact, you were a
lot of the fun in my childhood. I'm missing you so.

Miranda
I wish I'd known you better. I wish you hadn't gone.
May peace find you and surround you,
and may you know you are beloved.

CHAPTER ONE

ISABEL BARKER LIFTED her face and blinked hard at the silver skeleton and black waterproof cloth of her umbrella. As long as she didn't let the tears fall, she wasn't crying.

She was a fraud. A widow who wanted to throw herself on her husband's coffin, kicking and screaming—with rage. Each snowflake that smacked her umbrella was a drumbeat reiterating one word in her head.

Cheat. Cheat. Cheat.

She stared at the cheater's casket. Snow decorated the improbably polished mahogany with white lace and mixed with the tears of the real mourners who clustered around Will's open grave.

She wanted to scream the truth. Will had cheated on her. With her sister. *Her sister,* damn him—and damn Faith, too.

He and Faith had made a baby, despite the fact he'd always told Isabel he wasn't ready for children. Faith and Will had been trying to run away with eighteen-month-old Tony the afternoon they'd died in a car crash. It was the only explanation for the suitcases the police had found in the wreckage. Tony, miraculously safe in his car seat, couldn't explain.

Isabel turned her face away from Will's coffin, grateful that her nephew had survived. She couldn't look at her parents or at Ben Jordan—Faith's husband. Ben had also been Will's best friend. And Isabel's, too.

She hadn't looked at her family this morning when she'd seethed and mourned at her sister's service. Three months ago, after a day in the park with Tony, Isabel had asked Will again if he was ready for a child of their own. She'd tried to explain how much she longed for their baby. Instead of his usual "I'm too busy" excuses, he'd taken a deep breath and confessed to his affair with Faith.

Isabel had stared, disbelieving as the words flew like weapons. She'd begged him to say he was lying. He had promised he'd be faithful after an earlier affair at a time when their marriage had been young and troubled. She'd forgiven him then. He'd promised, after all.

And Faith—she'd never betray her own sister. Isabel lowered her head and pulled her umbrella closer to shut out the world. Fickle, beautiful, lucky Faith would never steal her little sister's husband and then pass off his child as her own and Ben's. She'd never ask Isabel to be godmother to her own husband's out-of-wedlock son. Faith had flaws, but she wasn't a monster.

A small groan escaped Isabel's lips. Ben leaned toward her, his shoes creaking in the early January cold. She felt guilty and eased away from him. Three months ago, she'd left town without telling Ben what Will had told her. If he'd done the same, she wasn't sure she could forgive him.

The minister lifted his hands. "Please bow your heads for a blessing." He hadn't strained himself with an extensive eulogy. Had the snow put him off? Or maybe Will, in a fit of regret, had confided in him, and he couldn't do an adulterous man justice.

Isabel stared at her black pointy-toed shoes and refused to pray. She'd abandoned Ben because she'd made herself a fool for Will, and she couldn't find courage or the words to admit how gullible and stupid she'd been. How straight-to-the-bone her husband's infidelity cut her even now.

They'd married straight out of college, and she'd worked as a copywriter for an advertising agency while Will became known for the innovative textiles he'd manufactured. After two years of phenomenal success, he'd decided he didn't want anyone to think his wife had to work. Isabel's job ruined his image as a provider and a philanthropist.

From the moment she'd resigned, the power balance between them had shifted. Bored stiff in her empty home, she'd thrown herself into any volunteer opportunity.

Will had approved of all efforts that got their

names in the paper, but he'd badgered her for time she should have devoted to him. When she'd said she might be a coat on a hook that he took down the second he came home in the evening, he'd reflected on that first affair, said she'd driven him to find someone who loved him the way she'd promised to—for better, for worse.

To hide mistrust she'd never overcome, she'd tried harder to be the wife he wanted.

What an idiot she'd been. Humiliation nearly strangled her. She'd never be dependent again, never try to please a man as part of some twisted love ritual. She'd never live another lie.

From somewhere inside, laughter came. Inappropriate, hysterical laughter. Fine time to take back the reins of her own life.

She swallowed with effort. She didn't need Will to tell her hysteria was unsuitable in a widow.

Ben must have thought she was choking. Taller by several inches, he looped his arm around her shoulders. She jumped. Once he knew what she'd kept from him, he'd never touch her again. He'd never trust her.

On her first day at the University of Virginia, Isabel had been carrying a mountain of clothes from her car to her dorm when she'd literally stumbled over Ben and Will repairing the VW bug they'd shared. They were already in their junior year.

Talk led to "chance" meetings that became dates

between her and Will. Always, Ben hovered at the edges, disappearing when appropriate, supportive when Isabel had feared Will might leave her for some other girl who'd thrown herself in his way. Will had been a flirt. A harmless one, Ben had always reassured her.

And then Ben had met Faith and they'd fallen in love, and the world had seemed perfect. Sisters who'd married best friends. Four best friends in all, who agreed to live in D.C.

Faith had discovered English Meadows, an "executive subdivision" of two-acre, green-beyond-belief estates in Hartsfield, Virginia. Ben and Isabel had tried to hold out against such a strong dose of well-to-do, covenant-laden suburbia. Big brick houses on small patches of grass.

Faith and Will had called them socialists in a capitalist world.

She glanced at Ben's dark-clad legs, all she could see of him with her head down. Had he noticed Will and Faith's stray looks of longing? Low-voiced conversations that only now seemed significant.

"Amen," said the minister.

A few women cried out loud. One man coughed, trying to hide his grief. Most of these people knew she'd separated from Will. They shook hands with Ben, barely muttering condolences her way before they bolted for their warm vehicles.

A line of cars snaked down a slithery path that

marked the snow-covered road on the cemetery's hill. Smoke rose behind gleaming black trunks, but distance and the brisk January wind buffered the engine sounds.

One woman seemed overwhelmed, trying to hide hushed sounds of anguish behind a white handkerchief. Another friend of Will's? Isabel turned away from her and teetered over the snow to take her mother's arm.

"Mom," she said, unable to comfort her with more. Amelia Deaver turned into Isabel's arms, burying a sob in her shoulder.

Her father caught her mom's waist. "Amelia," he said, his own voice husky. "Come on, honey. Let's go back to the hotel."

"Faith." Isabel's mother sobbed the name, and her pain finally made Isabel cry, too. She'd loved her sister. She would rather have fought her for Will than lost both of them. But she'd left, believing Will's claim that he'd found his one true love in her sister.

"Mom, let's go." They had to endure the reception at the Fitzroy Hotel, a central location for friends and employees. She pushed her mother's short wavy hair back. "You're shivering. You're going to get sick." The men in coveralls, hovering beneath the bare branches of a tree about a hundred yards down the road, weighed on Isabel's mind, too. She didn't blame them for wanting to finish their job in this weather, but neither did she want to watch them.

"I'm sorry." Her mother straightened, wiping her nose. "You've lost so much."

Isabel hated deceiving her mom. "I guess numbness protects you," she said. Three days had passed since the police had called.

"It won't for long." Amelia took her hand. "Where are your gloves, honey?"

Ben produced them from his pockets. "I found them on the ground beside the car," he said, handing them back.

"Thanks." Isabel took them without looking him in the eyes. "We'll meet you at the hotel." She glanced at her grieving mother. "Maybe you could bring Tony over to their hotel in the morning?"

"I wish you'd all stay at the house." Ben cupped her mother's elbow, and Amelia looked at Isabel's father. "George," Ben said, "don't you think you and Amelia would be more comfortable at my house than in a hotel?"

"I don't mind coming during the day, but I can't face Faith's things." Amelia dissolved in fresh tears. "I have to be able to leave when it gets to be too much."

"I was thinking of Tony," Ben said. "He needs his family around him."

"Is-a-bel." Amelia stuttered over her name. "Why don't you drive to the reception with Ben? Your things are still in your car, and he came with us. Afterward, you could stay at Ben's until Tony's better."

After that horrible conversation with Will, Isabel had fled to Middleburg, three hours away in horse country, where she'd found a job in an even smaller ad agency than the one where she'd worked after college. Because of the blizzard that was finally subsiding, she'd arrived this morning, barely in time for Faith's service.

But stay in her sister's house? Where her husband had no doubt made love to Faith? "I can't."

"What?" Her father's straight mouth turned down. "Ben's right about Tony needing us."

If Ben knew the truth about his son's birth father, he'd never let one of the Deavers near his child again. And Isabel, riddled with regret, hardly trusted herself not to blurt the truth, if only to relieve her own suffering.

"Don't make me—" She stopped as three pairs of eyes zeroed in on her. Her mother thought she should be more generous. Her father couldn't understand her selfishness.

God alone knew what Ben thought.

"Helping Ben take care of Tony will ease your mind about Will and Faith," her mother said. "Occupy your heart, sweetie."

"Mom." Her mother could be a little dramatic.

"I'd appreciate it." Dignity covered Ben in armor. He wouldn't cheat on his best friend. He'd never have looked at another woman. Even though she hadn't managed to fully trust her own husband, Isabel believed in Ben's loyalty.

And she owed him because she'd kept Faith and Will's secret.

"Okay."

"What?" her father said again. "No arguing?"

"You're right." She kissed her mother's icy cheek. "Thanks. I'll feel better, knowing you're with Tony."

Isabel longed to see the baby, but she dreaded entering her sister's house. "We'll see you at the hotel." She suspected they would try to leave as soon as they said hello, or they wouldn't be shoving Ben into her car. She hugged her father. "Will you come to Ben's in the morning?"

"Join us for breakfast, George." Ben seconded her invitation.

"Sounds good." Her father had eyes and concern only for her mom. He helped her over the slippery, uneven ground. His voice filtered back. "Maybe we shouldn't have asked Isabel to go. She's just lost her husband and her—"

"She lost Will three months ago," her mother said, loud enough to crash like cymbals around Isabel's head. "She began to mourn then."

Were divorce and death one to her mother? Will hadn't lived long enough to give her a divorce—or answers. Why—how—had he fallen in love with her sister?

"Isabel?"

She turned and finally looked at Ben, praying the truth wouldn't scream from her face.

He stepped away, his hands behind his back, his feet grinding loose gravel that barely covered the frozen mud. "What do you know?"

His question tied her tongue.

"I've been waiting for you to show up since the accident." Anger made his voice deeper, richer than she'd ever heard it. "Come on. I need the facts and you know them."

"Facts?" Stunned, she marveled at the act he'd put on in front of her parents.

"Tell me the truth."

"You must know." Three months ago, she'd been just as upset as he was now.

"You did know." He turned on his heel as if he didn't dare keep her within arm's reach. "You knew and you left without telling me."

"Why did you think I left?" There was so much hurt in his too-straight back she yearned to comfort him. She couldn't even offer a straight answer until she knew what he'd learned on his own. How could she be the one who told him the truth about Tony?

"You and I were friends." He faced her again. "I loved you—and Will. You walked out of my life and Tony's. You let me find out my wife had an affair with your husband." His eyes glittered. She'd never seen Ben cry. "You let me stumble onto the fact that Tony doesn't even belong to me."

What a hypocrite she'd been, moaning about betrayal. Her umbrella tilted in her hand. "I'm sorry."

"Who gives a damn about sorry?" Snow covered his black hair but melted on his face. Grief made him ugly.

"I thought I was dying for a while. I know I should have told you. I'd have felt betrayed if you'd left me living in a fake marriage, too, but I couldn't find the words or the way to tell you." His hard face didn't soften. She started toward the car. "Faith was my sister."

Ben pulled her to a stop. Her new black heels slid on the icy ground. She'd dressed to the teeth, and she intended to burn every stitch on her back as well as her purse and shoes. She was going to survive her husband's lies without one reminder of this day.

"I'll take you home so you can say goodbye to Tony." He all but bared his teeth in a snarl. "But you and your parents are no longer welcome in my house."

"I haven't told them, either."

"It's a matter of time."

"Stop manhandling me." A scientist rather than a salesman like Will, Ben hadn't perfected tact, but he'd never before carried a club. "If you keep us out of your house, people will notice something's wrong. And Tony's your son in all the ways that truly count."

"You say that because you feel guilty. Eventually, you'll realize you could raise your nephew. Do you think I don't know how badly you want a child?"

"I wanted my husband's child," she said, feeling stupid and gullible again as she admitted it. "I thought I had a marriage."

"You were trying to glue a broken marriage back together," he said. "Same as me."

"Did Will tell you that?" Damn him for trying to make her look bad.

"Didn't you fall in love with someone who lives in Virginia?" Ben stepped back, clearly restraining himself again.

"Will lied."

"He said you never wanted him. You turned him out of his own bed. You had an affair, and that drove him to Faith."

"I drove *him*." She hated the bewildered tears that threatened to shame her all over again. "Who are you going to believe? The man who slept with your wife, or the woman he also cheated on?"

"That's an excuse, Isabel. You didn't say anything."

"Because I didn't know how to warn you that you were living a lie? Did you ask yourself why I never called?"

"Will said you were probably avoiding Faith and me because Tony reminded you of the baby you wanted and didn't have. That you left him because he didn't want children. Then you turned to this other guy."

"If he said he didn't want children you know he was lying because he and Faith were taking their son."

Ben stared at her, frustration in every breath that misted around his face. Finally, he hauled her over the frozen ground. Because she hadn't wanted to hurt him, he seemed to be rattling the teeth out of her head. "Tony is my son." Fear glazed his blue eyes. "My child will never belong to anyone else. He never has."

"I've had it with men's egos." She hid behind her own anger. "Tony is my nephew. He's lost his mom. Even Will loved him, and he's gone, too." A sob caught in her throat. "That baby must be scared every time someone he loves walks out of a room. I won't give anyone an excuse to take him from you."

The cemetery workers walked into her peripheral vision. Isabel stared from the men to the mound of fresh dirt they were leaving behind.

Will had destroyed her sense of self. She doubted her own instincts. She'd never choose to live with another lie, but she hated that mound of dirt. She pushed her palm against her mouth to keep from crying out.

Ben held her other hand close against his beating heart. In that moment, she realized Will would never come back. He'd never smile at her or criticize or lie or ask what she'd made for dinner again. "Never" weighed upon her with the force of all eternity.

A woman could hate the man who'd rejected her, but she couldn't dance on his grave.

BEN HAD BARELY GLIMPSED the Deavers at the Fitzroy before they left. Isabel had worked the room on autopilot. She'd never remember a word anyone had said to her. As soon as decently possible Ben walked Isabel to her car. Unresisting, she let him help her into the passenger seat and then take her keys from her purse.

"I'll drive," he said, unsure she heard.

"Thanks. They were all kind, but I'm glad that's over. I swear I could hear the questions they didn't ask about Ben and me."

Despite hating her almost as much as he hated Will and Faith, he couldn't help wishing she didn't care enough to hurt like this. "How can you grieve for him?"

"I miss them both. I wish I would have happily divorced him and told her I never wanted to see her again, but I don't want them dead." She searched in her purse for a Kleenex. "Do you?"

"I'm not sure." Faith had left a note before she'd driven away with Will. She'd claimed Will had turned to her for comfort because Isabel had rejected him. If not for Isabel, they'd never have grown close enough to fall in love.

Even if it was true, was their adultery Isabel's fault? Shouldn't Will have fought for his marriage? Ben had known he and Faith had problems, but he'd never considered divorce.

Shutting Isabel's door, he walked along the side of the car with his hand on the cold metal. His best friend had made love with Faith and created the baby who slept in a crib down the hall from Ben's bedroom.

And Isabel had known. With a few words, she could take his son for her family. Eventually, she'd realize how badly he wanted to disappear with Tony.

He opened his door. Solemn and slender in her black dress and coat, her dark brown hair looped into a twisting chignon, she looked the part of a widow.

"Is my face dirty?" she asked. "Why are you staring?"

"I haven't heard from you since you went," he said, taking up where they'd left off before the reception.

"Now you know why."

"You say you love Tony. How could you cut yourself off from him?" He had to understand before he could trust her.

"I love him more than anyone." Isabel rubbed her pale cheek against one shoulder. "I'd been with him almost every day of his life until I found out the truth. He was like my own and Faith seemed to welcome my help. But after, I had to speak to her or you if I wanted to talk to him."

"You could have hung up if she answered the phone."

"I was mad at her, but I thought the second I heard your voice I might tell the truth."

Relief hit him so hard it hurt. "I wish you had

called. At least I'd have known in time to confront them. It was all over by the time I found out." With a shaking hand, he turned the key in the ignition.

"Because they're dead, Ben."

"I might have killed them."

"No."

He was glad she sounded so sure. It made him think he might stop being the man who hated everyone.

"How long are you going to hate me?"

"Hate you? You're all I have left." As insane as he felt, he had to keep her on his side. He craved a large meal of revenge, but he wanted his son more. He shoved the gearshift into Drive and eased away from the slushy curb.

Until two years ago, they'd lived in the same neighborhood. Out of the blue one day, Faith had insisted they move to a different subdivision, close enough to reach his office in less than an hour. He'd thought she'd liked its slight edge in upscale chic. Now, he realized she'd needed a little distance from her lover. Living so close to Will must have strained her acting abilities.

Half an hour later, Ben turned into the brick-lined entrance of his neighborhood. Isabel's car skidded as the tires lost traction in the snow.

He glanced at her, but her cynical smile, focused outside the vehicle, opened his eyes to the place where he lived.

Neat houses in neat rows, governed by rules and expectations that kept garbage cans and neighbors in their proper places. It looked pretty as long as no one peered inside.

He parked in front of the garage, and they both got out. Isabel's smile had faded. She clung to the door, obviously in the grip of second thoughts.

A plan came to Ben, fully formed out of distrust. "Come see Tony. He's still the baby you love." The nearer he kept Isabel, the better he'd know what she was thinking. "The reception was difficult. This is going to be impossible."

He opened the side door and waited. She stared at him and finally slogged through the snow, her head down, her breath coming so fast he could see her coat moving up and down with each respiration.

Faith's spotless chrome-and-granite kitchen stood empty. Isabel peered, anxious as a hunted animal. He'd always hated the cold kitchen. One small frame in Faith's picture of a perfect home.

He dropped his keys on the counter. "Wait here. I'll let the sitter know I'll take her home in a few minutes."

"Okay." But she glanced back at the door. She'd already proved her skills as a runaway.

He took a chance and left her there. He hoped she loved his son too much to leave. The sixteen-year-old girl from three streets over jumped off Faith's white leather sofa as he entered the family room.

"Mr. Jordan." She tended to watch adults like a spooked colt.

"We're back, Patty." He rarely understood adolescent girls, but he dealt with Patty by pretending it was normal for people to treat him like a burglar in the middle of a big job. "I brought Mrs. Barker to see Tony. Can you give us a few minutes and then I'll drive you home?"

"He's asleep." She scooped up her coat and book bag. "I can walk."

"Your parents would kill me." He looked out the wide bay windows. "The snow's getting heavier. I'll be glad to take you."

He headed back to the kitchen, more sure his jumpy sitter would remain than he was that he'd find Isabel where he'd left her. Miraculously, she'd waited.

His blood seemed to flow at light speed—a tremble in his fingers, a roar in his ears. Adrenaline. If he didn't hit something soon, his head might explode.

"Tony's napping." He tried to sound natural, but he felt as if he were outside his body looking down. "He won't wake up if we're quiet." He led Isabel to the stairs she'd climbed many times before.

At the top, his son's door stood partially open. Patty had stacked the baby's toys on a plain chest at the end of the too-ornate crib. Lamps that wouldn't survive a boy's first in-the-house football game lit the room with soft warmth.

Tony lay on his back, his arms and legs spread as if he were flying. Heat finally crept back into Ben's body as he watched Tony sleep. He hadn't lost everything in that accident. His son had survived. *His son.*

Isabel leaned on the crib's raised rail. She'd been in this house, bent over this crib, taken care of Tony almost as much as Faith.

She reached for the baby's hand but jerked her own back just before she touched him. Ben forgot for a moment that she'd let him believe in his fake life for three extra months. He started to remind her again she wouldn't wake Tony, but the harsh need on her face cut him short.

Tears floated in her eyes. Tony meant everything to her. Ben covered her hand and touching her felt right again.

"I know how you feel," he said. *But you can't have him.*

"I shouldn't have come. I thought I'd gotten used to not seeing him, but I was wrong." She splayed her free hand over her breasts. "He kills me, your boy."

Could he trust her? Until he was sure, he couldn't let her leave. He imagined himself in her place, watching her mother fall apart, her father walk around like a monolith without emotion. Isabel knew exactly what Amelia and George needed to get all better. And that was Tony.

He slid Isabel's hand off the crib and pulled her to the door. Without pausing, he took her to his room. Isabel caught the doorjamb, reluctant to enter Faith's domain of chintz and fussy swags.

"What are you doing?" she asked.

"Asking you to stay here."

"What?" She clenched her hands in the narrow skirt of her dress. "Just because Faith and Will slept together, you and I should try it? I don't need that kind of revenge."

At first, he didn't understand. "Are you nuts? I only brought you in here because I didn't want the babysitter to overhear." They'd been friends for most of their adult lives, and he was about to trick her into easing his paranoid fears. He couldn't help it.

For Tony. He'd risk everything, destroy anyone.

"Stay with us," he said. "Until you decide what you want to do next. The four of us were his family. As you said, he's lost Will and Faith. George and Amelia didn't get down here often enough for him to love them the way he does you."

She didn't even blink. It was as if she was saturated, had no more room to take in another shock. "You said you hated me."

"I was angry." Part of him did hate her. But would he have given up those three extra months for something as brutal as the truth? "Where else do you have to be?"

"In Middleburg. I have a job."

"What about your house?"

She blushed. Was she lying again? "I asked for time off to get the house ready to sell."

"Then stay here. You don't want the memories over there."

"No," she said in a cutting voice he didn't recognize. "I'd rather imagine Will and my sister here, in your bed." She took one look at it and ran.

The bathroom door slammed. He slumped onto a chair, his hands hanging between his knees. That bed was going out of this house tomorrow if he had to pitch it through a window.

He could hear water running. Isabel had to come out sometime. Meaning, he'd have another chance to win her over.

Guilt almost held him back. Even blinded by love for Faith, he'd recognized Isabel's softer heart. But distance might make her forget Tony wouldn't care how he'd been conceived. Ben loved his son too much to trust Isabel's good intentions.

The more she saw that he and Tony were the real father and son, the less willing she'd be to take him to court.

CHAPTER TWO

ISABEL LIFTED her head, saw herself in the mirror and jumped. Mascara-shadowed eyes, damp face, torment she couldn't hide.

No marriage. No sister. No best friend. No home.

She squared her shoulders. She was also no victim. Her life had changed forever, but she didn't have to hide in a bathroom, weeping over the past like a please-save-me heroine in a thirty-year-old paperback.

She yanked the door open. Ben, looking stunned, rose from one of Faith's big chintz armchairs. Isabel tried to go back into the bedroom, but she almost thanked him for coming into the hall before she could.

"What do you say?" he asked.

"Why do you care if I stay? You said this was my fault, too." He wanted something more from her than company for Tony. "What you're saying and what you want are out of sync."

"No marriage falls apart because of one person, and no relationship ends overnight." Confusion and guilt drained the life from Ben's face. "I worked too hard." His research kept him in his lab for long hours.

"Who knew you were leaving your home unde-fended?" Or that her husband would fall for her sister? "I never had a clue. Did I close my eyes to the signs?"

"All the stages of being cheated on," Ben said. "Bitterness and taking all the blame. But Tony doesn't have to be part of this train wreck."

"Why would you let me near him when you think I'm going to tell my parents we should take him away from you?"

His expression acknowledged the truth in her words, but the accusation quickly disappeared. Ben had learned to hide things, and his new talents made her uneasy. "The thought never crossed your mind?" he asked.

"I'm not like—" She stopped, lifting her hands to her unnaturally warm face.

"Like Faith?" he asked. "In what way? I'd like to know more about my wife."

So would she, but they'd both lost any chance at knowing who she'd really been. "I want Tony to be safe and happy. Faith and Will just wanted each other, and to hell with the rest of us."

Without touching her, he studied her face as if he were divining a mystery. "Stay with Tony until he gets used to being without his mom."

"I can't take her place." She turned away.

"Why don't you like people to see you cry?"

"Because I'm not weak." She looked back as if he'd forced her to. "I loved my sister—and Will—but I'm sick of being their joke. I imagine them laughing…."

"And you still think you love them?" Surprise raised his voice.

They both glanced toward the stairs. The babysitter could bring down Ben's shaky house of cards with one juicy conversation.

"You have to be more careful. Sixteen-year-old girls talk to their friends and their mothers. And her mother knows my mom from the parties you and Faith gave."

Ben pulled her closer. "You'd mind if your parents tried to take my son?"

"Why won't you trust me?"

"You had three months to tell me the truth."

"I was wrong."

He let her go, disillusioned. "At least you could have warned me they might take Tony and run. I almost lost my son."

Isabel had nothing to say. She couldn't be grateful that her sister's death had restored his child to Ben.

"Reading your mind is as easy as looking through a window," he said. "Everything you think is right there to see. I'm not glad she's dead, either."

"I can't believe it, even after today. My mom

hasn't even figured out what the bags in the car mean."

"What?"

"She thinks Will must have been giving Tony and Faith a ride to their place in Pennsylvania."

"He did that before when he had meetings in Pittsburgh," Ben said, but anger turned him into a stranger with dead eyes and a slitted mouth. "They told us he was taking her to your parents those times, didn't they? But they were together. Since cell phones, how would we have found out? I never called your parents'."

"I did, once or twice." She gave Faith and Will a grudging benefit of the doubt. "She must have gone home sometimes. She couldn't risk having you or me say something about those trips to my parents."

"Why do you make excuses for her?" His tone accused her of cheating, too.

"Faith was my sister." Will, she could condemn with less conscience, if only she could stop thinking she'd pushed him at Faith. She hadn't been able to tear down the wall she'd built after learning of his first affair, though she'd walked right through it into Will's arms just to prove she could.

"You think it was your fault," he said. "I know exactly what you mean. I'd like to forget either one of them ever existed, but I keep remembering the good times, too. Will was like my brother." It was his turn to look away. "And Faith gave me my son."

She hadn't meant to open a discussion about

auld lang syne. "I don't want to talk about them." She shook back her hair. "Look, my mother is Tony's grandma. She's the one who should help you take care of Tony."

"They've been around for three days and he's just starting to get used to them. He asks for his mom and you and Will. I don't know if it's because he only wants the three of you, or if he's actually scared of strangers right now."

"Strangers? I've never known you to be so dramatic, Ben. Tony's spent a lot of time with my parents."

"Apparently not as much as we thought." Unfamiliar arrogance frosted his tone.

"I haven't seen him for three months. He might not know me anymore." She eased away from Ben, aware she was about to infuriate him. "And how can I look at him without searching for some sign of Will?"

He didn't lose his temper. "Try to do what I do. Don't let yourself look for Will in Tony. Signs of him might drive you crazy." He rubbed his face. A five-o'clock shadow had begun to appear, right on time.

"I'm afraid." She stared at the nursery door. "I need to start my own life." She rubbed her hands together, cold and hot all at the same time. "What if I don't love him anymore because of Will and Faith?"

"I'm furious with you, Isabel, and even I don't think you'd blame an innocent child for Will's adultery."

And Faith's. Her sister's part in this filthy soap opera hurt almost more than Will's. Men could fall out of love with their wives. But then the wife was supposed to be able to parade her grievances past her sister for sympathy.

Ben took both her shoulders and forced her to look at him. "You and I are all that's left of the only family Tony's ever known."

"What do you mean you're furious with me? You don't act upset. Are you pretending?"

He let go too quickly. "I'm putting my son ahead of my feelings."

"But you have a plan." She saw him as she never had before. With that strange flat look in his eyes, his body strained to breaking point. "You let my parents drive you to the funerals. Would you have dragged them back here if I hadn't shown up?"

"You honestly think I'm planning something?" He looked embarrassed. "I'm not Will," he said, borrowing her earlier approach.

"I can't tell what's real."

He pressed both her hands to his chest. The weave of his wool suit against her palms made her feel again. She heard the low whisper of heat in the vents, noticed the faint lighting that softened the walls and lit her way—to Tony's room, or to the front door and freedom.

"I'm real. Tony's real," Ben said. "And you're his aunt."

"I can't do what you want." She wasn't being selfish. She was looking for salvation. "I want to know how people live when they're not surrounded by family and so-called best friends." Faith and Will would always pervade any moment she spent with her family—including Ben and Tony. She had to put what had happened behind her. "I'll send presents at Christmas and birthdays." Despite her best effort not to cry, the tears started again.

Ben mistook them for weakness. "You can't turn your back on Tony. He needs us."

"He needs you. And my mom and dad." Too many pictures went through her mind. Will, cuddling Tony, giving him piggyback rides. Resting his chin on the child's head while he'd smiled at her, always hiding the worst secret a man could keep from his wife.

Dying inside, she tried to push Ben away, but he took her hands again, and they stumbled inside his bedroom door. A whiff of Faith's perfume hit Isabel. Probably a memory.

"Anyone in my family would do for you," she said.

"Because they're Tony's blood relations? That's the kind of thinking that makes me believe you'll get over being angry with Will and Faith and then tell your mother and father about Tony."

"If I couldn't play God with you, how would I with them?"

"I'm your friend. They gave birth to you. They have nothing to do with the life you've led here. I'm a reminder."

She left him and opened the door to Tony's room. He followed. "Look at him," she said. "Why would I want to take him away from you?"

Ben crossed to his son's bedside. He pulled a blanket up to Tony's waist and tucked a ragged toy kitten beside him.

Tony's curly brown hair had grown longer. His sweet, plump hand curled in his sleep. Her feet moved of their own volition. She tripped on a stuffed hippo she'd never seen before. It squeaked and she glanced at the sleeping boy who owned her heart.

He was her flesh and blood, too. The thought—her need for him—frightened her. Just what Ben feared most.

Her nephew burrowed into his overstuffed comforter with a soft, sad sigh. "Mommy." He pulled his arms together in an empty hug.

She gritted her teeth and wiped her face. Tony's name screamed in her head. If she was ever good at being a mom, it would be because Tony had taught her to love like one.

Ben was right. How could her mother resist wanting to raise Faith's child? Having Tony so close would be like having part of Faith back.

Across the crib, Ben made a sound. The fear on his face frightened her.

"What?" she whispered, but she knew he'd read her thoughts again.

"Let's go." He pressed one hand to his son's back. "He needs to sleep, and I have to take Patty home."

He urged her out, but she hung back, gazing at her nephew. She'd do anything to protect him, and one thing she knew for sure. No good could come of tearing him away from his father. He belonged with Ben.

All their lives had changed, but Tony was a child. Only unconditional love and reassurance could keep him safe. She'd promised to take care of him.

"Let me shut the door." Ben nudged her out of the way and closed it, cutting off her view of Tony.

"What about Will's mom?" She spoke without meaning to. Her parents were dangerous enough, but Leah Barker wouldn't be able to stop herself from going after Tony if she discovered the truth.

"You'd tell her?" Ben obviously thought she'd lost her mind.

"Never." After her husband's early death from heart disease, Leah had raised Will as if he were her trophy. She wanted everything, but nothing ever filled her up. Nothing would ever be enough. "She'd take you to court if she even suspected Will was Tony's—" Isabel broke off, unwilling to utter the word.

Leah Barker had collapsed the second Isabel had phoned her. Leah had been the worst kind of permissive, overprotective, overfond mother, raising a son who'd never questioned his sense of entitlement.

"We can't let her find out." Ben spoke her thoughts exactly. Sudden relief relaxed his mouth and seemed to travel through his body on a shudder. "So you can't tell your mother and father." He tugged her toward the stairs. "My God, I don't understand the Barkers."

"I was one of them," she said. The name had filled her with pride on her wedding day. Leah had promised to be as much a mother as her own. Talk about a promise that couldn't be kept. But Will had chosen her to be his wife. With her parents, she'd always come second to Faith. She'd loved her sister and tried not to mind, but much of her new-wedded bliss had been built on gratitude to Will for putting her first.

What a fool she'd been.

Abandonment wrapped Isabel like a fine layer of the falling snow. She shivered, cold all the way to her soul.

Ben opened the sides of his jacket and pulled her into his warmth. Isabel held still, unwilling to make herself vulnerable.

"It's okay, Isabel. You can trust me."

Longing to believe, she pressed her face against Ben's shirt, reveling in his heat, in the comfort of her best friend's arms.

"You understand why we have to keep this secret?"

"When you talk like that, I can't trust you." She'd faced too much truth in the past three months.

Ben's heart thumped against her ear. "I can't help it. I haven't felt safe since I read that note."

Would she ever feel safe? "Do you trust *me*, Ben?"

"I saw what you looked like when you realized what you'd give up if you kept my secret. I can't trust you."

"Too bad for you if everyone can see straight through me." She didn't like her own bitterness.

"Would Amelia be able to put Tony first?" Ben tucked her head against him, and she suspected he didn't want to see her emotions. "Or would she tell herself Tony could learn to be happy with her and George? He might even forget me."

"Forget you?" Even to her, that image of the future was unbearable. "I'll do it. I'll help you."

Ben kissed the top of her head, his gratitude more real than either of their marriages had been. "Thank you, Isabel."

"Don't thank me. I'm sure lying is wrong. Look how it's already destroyed us."

FINALLY IN BED in the guest room, Isabel tossed and turned under crisp sheets and a down comforter. In darkness relieved only by an outside streetlight, she tried to shut off the accusations racing around her mind. There was no one left to accuse. Ben couldn't have kept Faith at home any more than she had Will.

Pounding her pillow, she lifted her head to stare at the clock—2:17.

Second, third and hundredth thoughts pulled her upright. She still wondered why Ben really wanted her to stay. She couldn't live with him and Tony forever.

He'd brought her bag upstairs before he'd taken the sitter home. After he'd left she'd returned to the baby's side, her heart melting into her shoes. Even knowing Will had been his birth father, she still loved Tony.

Why hadn't Will divorced her? She'd have given up rights to the business—any stake in his blessed bank account—to avoid a sentence in the hell he'd left behind.

Isabel jerked the bedding aside and turned on the lamp. Her sneakers lay on their sides by the closet. She stepped into them without bothering to tie the laces. Then she pulled a sweatshirt over her pajamas and opened the door.

Silence blanketed the dark hall. Ben and Tony needed sleep. After waiting a few seconds to make sure she hadn't disturbed them, she hurried down the curving stairs, snatched her coat out of the closet and then reached for the front door, her only thought, escape.

She glanced down at her clothing. The knife her husband and sister had slipped into her back was no one else's business. Wandering the neighborhood in her jammies would expose her and Ben, maybe even her parents, to ridicule and questions.

She turned, instead, toward the kitchen. When she opened the back door, the cold sucked the breath out of her lungs, but it felt better than smothering in her sister's home. If she didn't get fresh air, she'd need CPR.

Isabel stepped onto the deck and sank in snow that crept around the edges of her shoes. It felt good. She was alive if the cold could hurt.

But it really hurt. Damn. Suddenly she was also swearing at Will and Faith. And then at Ben for convincing her to stay.

Snowflakes wet her cheeks. She ran down the deck stairs and trekked through drifts to the gazebo where she and her sister had shared coffee, tea, secrets and each important milestone in Tony's life.

Last winter Faith had danced with her son in his first snow. He'd laughed as bits of ice bounced off his soft skin, and Faith had kissed each wet spot. Isabel gritted her teeth. Tony had lost a loving mother.

Faith's happiness that day had pricked at all Isabel's doubts. She'd trusted her sister enough to confide her worst fear—that Will might have found another woman.

Isabel hunched into her coat on the swing Will and Ben had hung from the ceiling. Her breath painted the air in front of her face. She exhaled again and watched the mist widen and then dissipate.

Faith had said she was being foolish. Her less-than-comforting response had hurt, but Faith had been right. No woman could have been more fool-ish or gullible.

"You'll freeze."

She jumped. "I didn't hear you, Ben."

"I didn't mean to scare you."

"It'd take a lot more than a guy in the dark to scare me tonight." She pulled one knee to her chest. "I'm spoiling for a fight."

"Yeah." He sat beside her, jostling the swing. "I'd like to punch someone, too." He'd positioned spot-lights around the yard, and their dim light colored his face pale blue.

"I'm sorry you had to find out with a note," she said. "I'm not sure I'd ever have found the courage to tell you, but I'm sorry you had to read about it."

"I knew something was wrong, but I never guessed anything about Will." He shrugged and the whole swing rocked. "I was lucky. Faith left the note in her makeup drawer. Amelia and George might have found it. They arrived the night of the acci-dent." He pushed his hands into his coat pockets. "Fortunately, I answered the phone when the morti-cian called about bringing her stuff."

"Good God."

"It was pretty awful." His silence echoed with pain. "Why did you wait so long to come?"

She stared into the dark, not wanting to answer, but how could he think worse of her? "I considered not coming at all."

"Really?"

She had shocked him.

"But Mom and Dad would have guessed something had come between Faith and me."

"And you wouldn't hurt them." He stopped the swing with his feet.

"You needn't sound suspicious."

"I'll be glad when your mother and father come over tomorrow and you don't tell them immediately."

"You hope that's the way it goes?" His doubts almost made her laugh. "You have to be kidding. If I wasn't able to tell you—when you were living the lie that changed me into a cynic—how could I tell my mom? She might feel better, but Tony would lose the last stable figure he's known."

"His father."

"His father, Ben. I agree with you."

The silence told her he doubted her. Just about the time she was getting angry, he nudged her elbow with his. "What are you going to do about the house?"

She pushed the swing back. "I don't think Will filed for divorce, and I was too busy finding a job. If the place still belongs to me, I'll sell it." She glanced his way. "Meanwhile, you have to decide if you want Will's half of our assets for Tony."

"Not a chance. I don't want anything from that bastard."

Cold crept through her coat and her pajamas.

"What if Tony needs the money when he's older? We're not talking a simple piggy bank. This is a lot of capital."

"Give it to Leah. If the truth comes out, she can decide whether she should help her grandson."

"I'm serious about not trusting Leah. I could turn over everything Will and I owned together and she'd still look for any crumbs I might have forgotten. She married into a mainline Philadelphia family, and she'll protect her name with her last breath. The more money to bolster her position, the better. You can't trust her finer qualities, Ben. You definitely shouldn't make Tony beholden to her."

"I won't touch a penny Will ever made—especially not for my son. I provide for Tony."

Isabel opened her mouth to suggest he wait until he wasn't so angry, but it was pointless. She didn't need his permission to ask her lawyer about creating a trust fund for Tony. "After I get out from under all this, I'm heading back to Middleburg. I love the horses and the trees and the farms. I'm not important enough to matter. No one looks at me with pity. No one expects me to be Mrs. Will Barker."

"We'll talk about your plans after you sell the house."

His domineering note struck a nerve. Will had always tried to steer their lives toward the image he wanted.

"You're upset." She tried to start out gently. "And

I've made it worse by talking about Will, but trying to push me around won't change anything for you."

The swing went forward and back. The metal chains sang a high-pitched, mournful tune until Ben stopped their motion.

"Don't talk about leaving now." He pushed the swing again, hard. "Please."

That "please" obviously cost him. She softened. "I won't." But was she falling into old habits? Trying to please a man whose gruff tone threatened to withhold affection? She gripped her armrest. "As long as you realize I'm no longer Will's amenable little wife. I was afraid he'd leave me, I guess, but I'd rather be left than play those kinds of games."

He turned to her. A stranger behind Ben's face who gave nothing away. Where was her old friend, loving, lovable, demonstrative Ben? "Thank you," he said.

She was right to doubt him. He wanted her here for some reason. She didn't understand, and she assumed it was going to hurt someday, but he might be correct about Tony needing familiar faces.

Ice crept between her collar and her neck. She shivered. From the snow? Or from doubts about Ben?

She turned toward the house, drawn to the faint glow of a night-light Faith had always left on in Tony's room.

Face it. In Ben's shoes she'd lie to keep Tony, and she'd keep on until someone caught her.

"I'd better go in," he said. "I don't like leaving him alone." Standing, he held out his hand. "You should come, too. If you fall asleep out here, we'll find you in an ice block in the morning."

She tried to laugh. "Ben, what if we came clean? We could work out visitation for everyone."

"Are you out of your mind? Didn't you hear what I said?"

"I'm willing to lie because it's best for Tony, but all the lies got us into this mess." Gut-sucking tragedy, she meant. "Wouldn't you have divorced Faith and been civil if she and Will had told us the truth?"

"After Tony came?" He started up the deck stairs. "I'd have killed her and buried her in the cellar, because I'd never have seen Tony again. And neither she nor Will would have believed they were denying me anything."

"Stop." If she hadn't known him better than she knew even her own parents, she might have believed in his threats. She grabbed his arm and pulled him back down. "I know you. Don't talk like that. You are not that kind of man."

"I want to be." Unshed tears weighted his voice. She wrapped her arms around his shoulders, refusing to believe in the bad man he was trying to become.

He held her off for a moment, and then his arms

came around her, almost too tight. Neither of them spoke, and she listened to his rough breathing. She'd been as angry as he was. It felt like sporting a cement foundation on your chest.

"Nothing hurts as much now that we're together," she said.

"I'm not so sure."

"Because I didn't tell you? If I could have asked you if you wanted to know, maybe I would have gone straight to you, instead of to Middleburg. I doubt it though. Will seemed surprised I was so hurt. Faith tried to call me a couple of times, but I never gave her a chance to speak. I kept hoping they'd realize how wrong they were, and they'd break off their affair. You'd never have to know."

He looked down at her with his stranger's face. "Do you believe that?"

She tried. If she could make herself believe, maybe she could convince him. But she was done with being an idiot, and he'd never let anyone past his suspicions.

"No." She stepped away from him. "And I'm cold."

"We don't have to pretend with each other," he said.

"They pretended to love us for years. That's why I hate the lies. I was blind to Will, and I don't want to be the same as he was."

"He must have loved you once."

"Because Faith loved you?"

He took her hand, but she'd bet it was an unconscious response. "Maybe she only used me to get close to Will. You were already engaged by the time she and I met."

"Hold on." Alarm bells rang in her head. "We can't let them make us think we're not worth loving, and I won't turn into one of those women who refuses to trust because one man cheated on me." Another lie. She hadn't fully trusted Will since he'd first strayed. She tugged her hand out of Ben's, more interested in standing on her own two feet.

Ben let her go. "I'm more worried about being so angry I make Tony forget how to be happy."

"You're a good dad. You won't do that."

"Thanks, Isabel." He took the first two stairs in one stride. "I needed that."

He seemed to feel better, but she noticed the beginnings of a headache and a thick coating of ice in her shoes. Too many moral questions to ponder around here.

"What are you going to do in the morning?" he asked.

"Start on the house." A labor that would have unmanned Hercules. "I have to sort our things."

"Let me help. Make a list of what you want to keep and we'll go through the rest."

"You don't owe me, Ben." She caught up on numb feet. "The ghosts in that house are mine to face."

Ghosts of Will doing his finest imitation of a loving husband. Faith—with whom she'd played dolls and dress-up, made Christmas and birthday presents for their parents, shared secrets and fights—Faith, taking her place.

Isabel fought an urge to wrap her arms around Ben and bury her face in his shoulder. She needed courage to face the home that had no doubt become her sister's over the past three months.

CHAPTER THREE

ISABEL WOKE, groggy from lack of sleep. Tony's crying pulled her to her feet, but then she heard Ben's comforting voice, and Tony laughed. Isabel sank back, dragging a pillow over her face.

It all came back. Her sister and her husband had found the love Will had apparently never been able to feel for her. They'd had Tony together. They'd run away, only Tony surviving in the wreckage they'd left behind.

Tony. Her nephew. Her husband's child. Leaving would be so easy.

Except she loved Tony with a mother's heart. None of this was his fault, and Will had already ruined enough of her life. She might never learn to forgive Faith, but Will's falseness wasn't about to destroy her love for Tony.

She tossed the pillow toward the headboard and climbed out of bed. First, a shower that felt more like baptism into a crazy, borrowed existence. Then she put on jeans and a snug green sweater and began to unpack the bag she'd left in the middle of the floor last night. Thank goodness, she'd brought enough clothing to take her through selling her house.

She was hanging her things in the closet when Ben knocked on the door. "You awake?" he asked softly from outside.

"Come on in." She looked for Tony, but Ben came alone.

He held out her cell phone. "Leah."

Great. One free breath would have been nice before she had to face her former mother-in-law. "How'd you explain my staying here? She doesn't know—"

He put his hand over the phone. "She knows you were separated. Why would you stay in that house? And why are you trying to protect Will?"

"He was still her son."

Ben looked disgusted as he passed the cell.

Isabel replaced his hand with hers, blocking their voices again. "What did you say?"

"Hello, and that I'd find you."

Maybe she was overreacting, but she wasn't used to this angrier version of Ben. "I'm sorry. She— I know she can be awful, but she loved Will."

"As long as he stayed in line."

"She loved him as much as she can love anyone." She brought the phone toward her ear.

"Wait." Ben held out his hand. "Tony's downstairs. He must have seen you last night because he keeps calling for you."

"I'll come down." Armed with her last ounce of nerve.

"Thanks. He'll feel better after he knows you're here."

She hoped Ben was right. They might be setting Tony up for another loss, because she had to find her own life soon. She couldn't linger forever on the edges of Ben and Tony's.

She spoke into the phone. "Leah?"

"I thought you'd hung up. What took so long?"

"Ben and I were talking about Tony. How do you feel now?"

"Exhausted. I know people are going to talk because I didn't show up, but I can't manage to get out of bed yet. Are you going to visit me, Isabel? I'd like to hear about my son's service."

Leah must be delirious. "You want me?" Despite her claims to be Isabel's second mother, Leah had treated her as if Will had married the hired help.

"We're all that's left of my son now. We must help each other through our grief."

"Huh?" The many dramas of Leah Barker annoyed the hell out of Isabel, but she bit her tongue. "Calm down, Leah. I'll come up to Philadelphia in a few weeks, but I have to close the house first."

"The house? Doesn't it belong to Will?"

"You haven't changed that much."

"Pardon me?"

Isabel almost laughed at Leah's stronger, affronted tone. "You're protective," she said, "of Will. I'll let you know what the attorney says about the house."

"And everything else."

Just like that, her attitude wasn't so funny. Isabel still owned the things she'd brought into her marriage. "You have nothing to worry about, Leah."

"Why are you staying at your sister's house?"

Just the question to turn the knife in Isabel's wounds. "Ben asked me and I want to spend time with Tony."

"Don't you care what people will think? After all, you and Will were separated."

"What are you implying, Leah?"

"I'm worried about my son's reputation. You should be, too. I know you had problems, but he loved you."

That bastard. He'd probably fed his mother the same story he'd given Ben—that Isabel had cheated on him. He'd never realized he didn't have to hide his flaws from Leah. She refused to see them anyway. Eventually, he'd have persuaded her Faith was a victim he'd saved from a bad marriage, too.

"I loved Will, Leah. Let's leave it at that. I need to get off the phone and go start on the house."

"If I come stay with you, will you move back in?"

The threat didn't scare Isabel. Leah hadn't even come to her beloved child's funeral. She'd hire an attorney before she'd travel all the way to Virginia to grab her share of Will's belongings.

"Sure," Isabel said. "Let me know when you're coming."

Her mother-in-law was silent for several seconds, no doubt planning her next offensive. Isabel smiled. "You'll fill me in on what you're doing?" Leah took another tack. "You should call me each evening."

"I'll have Ray Paine give you an update."

"Ray? He's Will's attorney."

"And mine, and I wish you wouldn't crowd me, Leah."

Again, she fell silent. "Let's not argue, honey. We won't pretend I didn't think you were wrong for Will. Maybe I was right, maybe not, but you're all I have left of my boy, and I don't want to lose you. Maybe I'm trying to make sure you don't cut all ties with me."

"By accusing me of burglary?" Any non-succubus would know that was a mistake.

"I don't want you to cut me out. I have the right to make demands." The bubble of her arrogance deflated. "I hate situations I can't control."

A family trait. "I don't like people who try to manage me. And being called a criminal puts me off, Leah. Why don't you say what you mean instead of playing games?"

"Would you believe me if I told you how much I care about you?"

Care seemed like a strong word for what Leah appeared to feel, but she was trying to preserve their tenuous connection. Will must not have told Leah the "Isabel cheated" story after all. Leah would never forgive disloyalty to her son. "I might suspect you had an ulterior motive."

"I do care. I'm protective of my son's things, but you were part of his life. I wish I'd been nicer to you while you and Will were married."

Leah had stopped making sense, but Isabel couldn't turn her back on Will's mother. Grief could make a woman talk crazy. "Don't worry, okay? I won't take anything that belongs to Will, and I won't disappear without telling you."

"You're the only person I can talk to about…"

"Shh, Leah. Don't upset yourself. Is anyone staying with you?"

"Janet's here." A friend who'd shown her the ropes of being a popular Philadelphia wife. Janet had never liked Isabel, either.

"Go do something with her awhile. Something that takes some energy."

"You mean like shopping?"

Isabel laughed. She'd had silver polishing or cooking breakfast in mind. "Whatever keeps you busy. You don't have to deal with everything today. Work your way into getting used to—" She couldn't say Will's death. "To what's happened."

"I think you're right."

It never took much work to persuade Leah to pamper herself. "I'll call you later."

"Thanks. And I'm grateful for the advice, too. We'll talk soon. I still wouldn't mind knowing what you plan to do about my son's things."

Leah couldn't stop, and Isabel wasn't a saint. For now a call was the best she could offer.

"POCK, DADDY, POCK!"

Which translated to *Take me to the park across the street, Dad.* Ben wiped cereal off the wall and picked more out of Tony's hair. "Just a minute, Son. Let me chisel the kitchen clean first."

At least he'd stopped begging for his "Iz-bell."

Just as Ben wiped the last splat of cereal off the counter behind Tony's high chair, Isabel came into the kitchen, like a woman taking possession of enemy territory.

"Morning," she said, her cheerfulness obviously an act.

How had Leah put her in this mood?

"My Iz-bell." Tony kicked so hard the whole chair rocked. Ben and Isabel reached for him at the same time.

"Let me." Her eyes, soft with love, distracted Ben. His house felt starved for love.

Isabel eased his cooing son out of the high chair. Tony wrapped his legs around her as if he were either wrestling or claiming her for all eternity.

"I love you, baby." She said it with wonder. That was the worst thing about cheating spouses. They made you forget what kind of person you were.

"You really thought you could stop loving him?" Ben's throat tightened as Tony planted a wet, cereal-specked kiss on Isabel's cheek. She looked at Ben, eyes wet.

The heavy air inside his house seemed to lighten.

"I'd better take him." Ben reached for his boy. "You're still going out?"

Nodding, Isabel stared at Tony as if she couldn't get enough of him. Giggling, Tony burrowed his face into her hair. "He's fine, despite what he must have seen in that accident." She hugged him again until he wriggled. "You can have him in a sec, and then I have to call Ray before I go."

"Why?" He didn't want to hear anything more about this legacy idea. He wet a paper towel with warm water and tried to clean some of the detritus his son had rubbed on her cheek and neck.

The way she set her stubborn jaw equipped him with plenty of elbow grease. "I want to discuss setting up a trust fund for Tony, and while I was talking to Leah I realized I'd better find out for sure about my legal rights."

"Don't think you can run over me about Will's money. No one provides for my son except me."

"Be sensible. You can't see the future. Who'd have believed three months ago that all this was waiting for us? When Tony grows up, he might need—and want—Will's legacy."

"Will always said you hated business matters." He closed in again, trying to finish the cleanup.

"What Will actually meant was that he hated for me to ask questions about the business. He felt I was challenging his role as the great provider." She dropped the sarcasm. "Another reason to feel idiotic for trusting him. I may be penniless." She freed one hand and pushed his paper towel away. "What are you doing to my face?"

"Cereal." He scrubbed off the last grains and then showed them to her. "Tony shared with you."

"Is it in my hair, too?" But when she turned to let him search the brown strands, Tony grunted and tightened his legs.

"My Iz-bell, Daddy."

"Aunt Iz-bell," Ben said for maybe the billionth time.

"Uh-huh." Tony nodded with vigor. "*My* Iz-bell."

They had bigger problems. Someday Tony would grasp what *aunt* meant. "Okay, buddy. Let's finish cleaning you both before your Iz-bell has to hose herself down."

"No." Tony resented even a paper towel coming between them. Ben had to laugh. Otherwise, his boy might tempt him to cry. "I told you he's lost too many people lately."

"Ben." Without warning, Isabel put one arm around him.

She seemed too close. He couldn't get enough air. What the hell had his voice betrayed? As his lungs screamed, he let her hold him, and he was almost as grateful as his son.

This was good, he told himself, even as he hated the devious path his thoughts took. She wouldn't hug him if she didn't feel attached. The more attached he made her feel, the safer he and Tony would be.

But he must have hugged back too tightly. Tony began to squeal, and Isabel laughed, moving away.

"I guess we needed that." She picked up Tony's bowl from the table and set it in the sink. "It's been too long for all of us."

Fighting remorse that was pointless, since he'd have used any innocent, unsuspecting soul to keep his son, he followed her to the sink. "More cereal." He smoothed it out of her hair and ran the paper towel over his son's face, to Tony's squirming disgust. "And we're all ready to go."

"Go where?" Isabel asked. "I mean where are you and Tony going?"

"The park, if you don't want our company." He tossed the paper towel into the garbage can as the doorbell rang.

Isabel turned with a wary look that reminded him she really had been through the same experience that had changed his life. "I was surprised no one brought the traditional casseroles."

"I asked them not to." How else did a guy act when his wife died, leaving a brief, informative note about her affair? "I don't know if she told anyone else the truth. Every time one of her friends shows up I'm afraid something will happen that makes me lose Tony." He circled Isabel and his son, heading for the front door. "Those damn suitcases, for instance."

"I know. I plan to repeat Mom's theory about Will giving Faith and Tony a ride to her and Dad's house." Annoyance tightened Isabel's voice.

"I'm glad you told me. It's a better excuse than anything I came up with."

"Have you considered a DNA test?" Isabel asked.

He turned back, bleak. "I won't leave a trail of evidence that proves I have questions about Tony's paternity, and Faith's affair explains why my marriage had turned into an endurance test." He looked miserable. "I can't make myself prove my son belonged to another man."

"He never will."

Isabel's desperate comfort provided little relief. He passed through the dining room where the table was still set for Faith's next dinner party, and entered the hall. He reached for the door, wishing he could plaster a do-not-disturb sign to the other side.

George and Amelia were on the threshold, George taking a quick scan of the neighbors, Amelia clinging to his arm as if she might sink without his assistance. "You're exhausted." She was one to talk, with her grayish hair flying from a bun he'd guess she hadn't repaired since yesterday. "I knew we shouldn't leave you alone. You have too many memories in this house." She peered over his shoulder. "Where are Tony and Isabel? Not awake yet?"

"It's almost ten," George said. "No kid sleeps this late. Have you eaten, Ben? We thought we'd take the family out for breakfast."

"I'll give Tony his bath and dress him for you, Ben," Amelia said. "And maybe later we could take him to the park."

"I've already dressed him. We painted the kitchen with cereal, and we're headed to the park." Aware he owed Isabel a random act of kindness here and there, he prepared the path for her to go her own way. "Except Isabel has some work to do at her house."

"How is she this morning?" Amelia pushed past him. "Isabel?"

"In the kitchen, Mom."

Her happy voice startled him.

"There she is." Amelia rewrapped a striped scarf around her throat. "We'll all visit the park. We'll get a bite to eat and then work it off on the baby swings. I'd love some fresh air."

"Are you nuts?" George took his wife's arm. "In that skimpy overcoat, you'd freeze in minutes."

"It gets colder than this in Philadelphia."

"And you huddle by the fireplace every time it snows." He nodded toward Ben. "You go. Amelia and I will say good morning to Isabel and then find ourselves some breakfast and a paper. We'll bring something back. Maybe those doughnuts Tony likes."

"You don't have to leave because Tony and I are going out. Come on into the kitchen. I have coffee and a paper, George."

"Don't want to make a mess of your kitchen." George prowled like a caged animal under his daughter's roof. "We'll see Isabel and then go our own way. Besides, Amelia likes her own copy of the crossword puzzle."

"I never—" Amelia began, but George's strange expression stopped her from finishing.

Ben closed his own eyes, swearing a blue streak in his head. Faith might have followed Will's lead and told her father some god-awful story. Always a daddy's girl, she wouldn't have been able to run out on her marriage without trying to swing her father onto her side.

George often told his girls they were the best things that had ever happened to the world. According to Faith, he'd never been able to live with flaws, so she'd always tried to hide hers. George would *have* to convince himself Faith was blameless. Her affair, and then passing Tony off as Ben's child. Her actions would have forced George to take sides between his two girls.

For Isabel's sake as well as his own, Ben prayed he was wrong and Faith hadn't found the guts to confess. "Isabel, your mom and dad are here."

They found her with the top of Tony's high chair up, wrestling him into his coat.

"I'll do that. He hates it."

"I used to know the tricks." Isabel gave up and hugged both her parents. "Did you sleep well, Mom? You look tired."

Ben concentrated on Tony, pulling up his hood and tying the laces in a bow. Tony pushed at his hands with his usual resistance.

"We slept fine." Amelia backed away from her to study the room. "Isn't this kitchen lovely? It could be a show home, Ben."

Isabel leaned against the sink and he tried not to notice her white-knuckled grip on the granite counter. "It's lovely," she said with magnificent blandness.

"Amelia." George pulled her close and kissed her temple. "You're being tactless."

"I'm not comparing you to your sister, Isabel." Amelia breathed deep. "I'm looking for signs of Faith. I miss her so much."

Isabel forgave immediately and hugged her mom

again. "It's all right. I do understand." But her bleak expression told a different story.

Ben wished he could pull her away from her mom, but that would draw attention to the two of them being in some bad situation together. He couldn't afford to make the Deavers look more closely for the reasons their other daughter had been in that car with their son-in-law.

Isabel moved away from her mother with the excuse of returning Tony's mitten. "Mom, are you and Dad going to the park with Ben and the baby?" She held the glove for Tony and he slid in his hand.

Ben watched, bemused. Her way was much better than his usual method, all but pinning his boy to the floor. And he still rarely maneuvered Tony's thumb into the right spot.

"We haven't eaten breakfast," George said again.

"Too bad. You could both use the exercise after being cramped in cars and hotel rooms."

Ben lifted Tony, absently kissing his forehead for the sake of keeping close contact. "You know you're both welcome to stay here." The last thing he wanted was the two of them in constant watch mode, but now that Amelia had said she couldn't sleep surrounded by Faith's memories, he offered without fear she'd accept.

"Thanks, but we tend to talk at night when we can't sleep, and George wanders. He'd only annoy you."

Amelia kissed Tony's forehead, too. Appreciative of all the attention, Tony wrapped his arms around his father's head.

"If you're sure." Aware of Isabel's heavy suspicions, he was ashamed of playing both her and her parents. Last night, his plan had seemed like a good idea. When she decided to tell her parents everything about Faith and Will he'd know. The change in her would be as obvious as the twirl of a weather vane.

"I'd better get this little guy out of here." Ben tried to pull Tony to a less tipsy position, but Tony liked perching above the world. He thumped Ben's head, a small, mischievous snowman playing a convenient drum. "We may drop by the house later, Isabel, to see if you need any help."

"Would you like a hand, Isabel?" Her mother's anxious question softened Isabel's glance.

"I have to do it all myself. Even if you could help, I'd have to look over everything first, because some items go back to Leah."

"How is she?" George didn't sound as if he really cared. As easy to read as his daughter's, his tone asked how any woman could take to her bed rather than saying a last goodbye to her son. "On her feet again?"

"Dad." Isabel said no more. They'd obviously discussed—even argued—about George's attitude toward Leah.

To his shame, Ben felt a little satisfaction that Isabel and her parents weren't entirely in sync.

CHAPTER FOUR

"RAY?" ELBOWS DEEP in a wardrobe full of sweaters, Isabel almost dropped her cell phone. She grabbed it as it slid off her shoulder. "This is Isabel Barker."

"Isabel." Ray's welcome-back-to-town was unconditional and uncomplicated. "I tried to speak to you at the funerals, but you were so upset I'm not sure you saw me."

She hadn't. "I'm still troubled." That was no lie. "I need to see you about legal matters between Will and me."

"I'm glad you called. We do need to talk. Can I send you back to my receptionist to make an appointment?"

"I wish you'd meet with me today, Ray, if you can."

He hesitated only a second. A long-ago friend of Will's dad, he'd been more a father figure to both Will and her than an attorney. "Come now if you don't mind talking over my lunch."

"Thanks. I'm grateful."

About twenty-five minutes later, she turned into the parking garage at Ray Paine's marble-and-glass building off Dupont Circle. Hardly anyone noticed her as she padded across the polished entrance in sneakers. Designer sneakers that would fall apart at the first hint of a run, but still…

In the elevator, she punched the number for Ray's floor. Determined to be strong from now on, being here reminded her how she used to fade into her husband's background. She dreaded the receptionist's greeting.

The woman had always had a soft spot for Will. The way she reacted to Isabel would show immediately whether Will had talked to Ray about a divorce. Isabel braced herself for open antagonism.

Her angst came to nothing. The doors opened on Ray's private floor, and the receptionist's desk stood empty in front of his open office. Isabel checked the hall. Up here, she'd be underdressed in jeans and a sweater.

Who gave a damn how she looked? She should have asked for this meeting before she'd scuttled off to Middleburg—hiding as if she'd done something wrong.

"Isabel? Is that you?"

Ray came out. Tall and spare and silver haired, he opened his arms. "I knew I heard the elevator. How are you?"

Relief swept her. Nothing had changed. Ray still loved her without resentment, which meant Will had kept his mouth shut. She'd have to explain. Telling him about her sister and her husband wouldn't be easy, but at least Will hadn't treated their friend to his cover story about her straying first.

"I'm okay, considering." She hugged the older man, who offered a second squeeze for comfort. "Thanks again for seeing me."

"Why haven't you called? I can't remember how long it's been." He looked closer. "Are you sleeping well?"

She stepped away. "I'll be better after you and I talk. Have you finished eating?"

"Don't worry about that." Curiosity lifted his plush eyebrows. "You know me—work through lunch every day. Come in and we'll talk. I'd absolutely *love* to share my salad."

Despite their mutual sadness, Isabel found a smile for his sour tone. "You offer it as if you're suggesting cyanide."

"I hate the stuff, but Pam tells me I'm thickening at the middle." He patted his stomach, but his grin turned sheepish as if humor might be improper. After all, she was a widow.

She just didn't know how to grieve. "Pam?"

He glanced toward the receptionist's desk. "My—uh—"

"Oh." Pam must have a general weakness for powerful men. "You don't look thick to me."

"Ah, you're a good friend. Your company will help the greens go down easier."

Isabel followed him inside and sat carefully on a

black leather armchair across from his perch on the
edge of a matching sofa. With a plastic fork, he
picked through a mound of salad in a take-out box.
"We should discuss the will first."

"I'm still in it?"

He looked up, eyebrows twitching. Spinach
dropped off his fork. "Why?"

She touched her temples, fighting dizziness. "You
didn't know we were separated?" His welcome-
back-to-town hadn't been that at all. He hadn't realized she'd left.

Ray worked out the changes in his head. She'd
like to hear his thoughts out loud. What did this alter?

"Will never told me—and I might add, neither did
you." He dropped the fork and sat back, sliding his
hands along the leather cushion. "I'm dumbfounded.
When did this happen?"

"Three months ago. Will told me he'd fallen in
love with—someone else, and I left our house. I've
been in Middleburg since then."

"You're kidding." He plucked steel-rimmed
glasses off the coffee table and pushed them onto his
nose. "Will never mentioned it. He made several
appointments with me. Never said one word." He
waited for her to fill in the gaps.

"I'll never be able to explain anything he did." Her
confusion only mortified her. "Why did he see you?"

"Business. Contracts he wanted me to check. A
complaint against your home-owner's association.

He wanted to build a pool, but the architectural review board turned him down. I thought it was supposed to be a surprise for you."

Faith's voice whispered childishly in Isabel's head. She remembered a night in their tent in the backyard. "When I grow up, I want a pool I can swim in every day," Faith had said. Isabel had wanted a horse.

Naturally, Faith's lover, who'd thought horses a waste of money and time, since he wasn't going to play polo or learn to jump, had tried to put in a pool for her. They must have planned to share Isabel's house. She resisted a sharp surge of pain. "You're still my lawyer, too?"

"Do you want someone else to represent you?" Ray looked unhappy, which Isabel took as a good sign from a successful attorney.

"Not at all. I plan to cling to all the friends I can salvage."

"I am your friend, Isabel. Maybe that's why Will didn't tell me. I was never likely to side with him."

She frowned and tried to talk over a catch in her heartbeat. "Never? Are you saying he had other women before—this one?" He didn't know yet that Will had loved her sister.

Ray shoved the salad farther onto the black marble table and stood. "I can't believe Will had an affair."

"I'm more surprised he didn't tell you. I've been expecting divorce papers in the mail."

"I'm not a divorce attorney, Isabel. And Ben had the good sense not to mention marriage or divorce." He looked disgusted. "Don't tell me the woman's name. I've had enough of human nature, and I don't want to be disappointed in anyone else I've cared for. Let's get back to the estate."

"Are you sure you can be fair now that you know the truth? I don't want anything of Will's, just what belongs to me."

"You're his prime beneficiary, and you're in charge of his estate, Isabel. Everything he owned comes to you."

"No." She rubbed her chin against one shoulder. "Will was never that careless, and I'm not comfortable, considering we'd separated when he—at the time of the accident." But this was an opportune moment to bring up Tony. "I have to tell you something I don't want you to pass on to anyone else. Including Pam."

"She's not a paralegal."

"I have to tell you about the other woman."

"Are you sure?" He resettled his glasses, steeling himself for the worst. "I don't know what's wrong with me. What are you going to tell me that I haven't seen in my career?"

"It was my sister, Faith."

"My God."

Because none of her emotions were working as they should, she smiled, stunned to be the calm one.

"I can't thank you enough for being on my side, but brace yourself for more."

"More? What else could they do?"

Ben wouldn't want her draping his dirty laundry all over Ray's thriving office. It brought her no pleasure, either.

"Faith's son, Tony, is actually Will's natural son."

"Will's natural..." Ray linked his fingers as if he were praying. "That boy's got to be a year and a half old."

Meaning they'd been seeing each other for-damn-ever. "Exactly. I'd like you to separate everything as if we had divorced."

"Because you want to give it to your husband's illegitimate child? I can't." He spun away from her and ended up at his desk. He picked up a crystal globe on a plinth and then replaced it. Likewise, an ornate marble-colored pen and pencil set on his desk. "I won't give your future away."

"Tony is Will's child, Ray. None of this is his fault, and I love him, too. He's my nephew. I can't cheat him out of his inheritance."

"How do you know all this? When did Will tell you?"

"Three months ago. That's why I left. And then Faith left Ben a note."

"A note?" He scoffed with a lawyer's disdain. "I'll need DNA results before I consider doing what you're suggesting."

"No test." She had to follow Ben's wishes. No trace of the truth for anyone to find. "I believe what Will told me. And Faith wouldn't have lied to Ben when she was leaving him."

"She might have, to keep him from sharing custody of her child. I know you loved her, but you never saw—the two of you had different kinds of hearts. Yours is soft. Hers was selfish."

"Not completely. She loved her son. She apparently loved my husband, too. Who knows what made her the kind of woman she became? I wasn't happy in my marriage, either."

"How can you be so calm?"

"I'm not. Inside, I'm working hard at not screaming my head off, but that wouldn't help anyone."

He went back to the sofa. "You don't have to prostrate yourself on their graves."

"I've prostrated myself for the last time for Will Barker." She regretted every decision she'd ever made with her husband's comfort in mind. "This is for Tony."

"I can't believe Ben will accept anything from the man who cuckolded him."

Rage filled her for a second. She didn't want anyone saying that about Ben. It made him seem weak, and he was proving his strength with each passing moment. She pushed Ray's salad back to him, but he only made a face at her.

"He doesn't want the money, but it belongs to

Tony. He might need it someday. If Will had been thinking like himself, he would have changed his will in his…son's favor." She couldn't love Tony more, but she hated his parents a little when images of them together taunted her.

Ray refused to give in. "Think about what you're doing. This money may sit in an account untouched forever if Ben doesn't want Tony to have it."

"I'm not quite sure how to put this, but if it's mine, and Tony's my nephew, it'll go to him someday, no matter what Ben wants."

Ray leaned forward and stabbed a piece of romaine so hard his fork skewered the container. "If that idiot Will had been himself, he'd have remembered who he had waiting at home."

She didn't want anyone saying nasty things about Faith, but how nice to have a champion. "You're turning into my hero." Tears welled again. She was sick of wanting to cry—bound to rust into immobility if she kept this up. "I need to remake my will and leave everything of Will's to Tony. Do that right away because, apparently, you never know when you might die."

He didn't flinch at her black humor. "I won't mention again that you're under no legal obligation. You're obviously determined."

"I'm thinking on the fly, but I don't want anyone questioning Tony's parentage. Make sure you refer to Tony as Will's and my nephew. Ben's afraid my parents or Leah will try to take Tony away from him. We cannot let them find out."

"My God," he said again. "But your parents have more legal right to Tony."

"This isn't about legal standing. I don't think it's good for Tony to be ripped out of his father's home at eighteen months." She watched the implications unfold in his mind as his frown deepened. "You're keeping my secrets now."

Ray reached for the notepad and pen on the table beside his salad. "I'll think of a way to do it."

"Be careful."

"I didn't plan to get in touch with the media." He gave her a wry look. "The world couldn't care less how Ben raises his son."

"Thanks, Ray. I know I'm paranoid, but I'm hoping you'll catch enough of my irrational fear to make sure Ben and Tony don't get hurt."

"Don't worry about me." He looked around his office. Success shone from every gleaming surface.

Standing, she leaned across the table, and he got up to hug her. "Will you call me when you're ready to talk?" she asked.

"As soon as I finish the paperwork for your will, I'll put together a plan for a trust fund. We'll talk about what comes next. You'll need to ask Ben to join us."

"He told me not to do this. I don't think we can count on him going along with what I want."

"Just ask him to come in and listen. He doesn't have to agree."

"I'll ask, but he's a proud man." She didn't mind exposing her doubts. "He doesn't want anything from Will and I guess he figures Will already took plenty from him."

"We have to make him see Tony's entitled to everything you're trying to give him."

Ray ushered her from his office. She was just as happy to escape before Pam showed up.

By the time she turned into her own neighborhood, she was so antsy her skin seemed to be jumping. English Meadows had suited Will's idea of what his home should be. Each house in its own brick-fenced island. Each neighbor intent on his privacy. For her it had been like living in a fishbowl.

One of the neighbors, who was a one-woman Neighborhood Watch, had always been friendly, but she'd liked to know what went on behind everyone's walls.

Isabel opened the gate with a remote she'd forgotten to leave the day she'd moved out. She parked in the curving driveway, in front of the door.

As she climbed the stone steps, a black bird flew off the iron table that was flanked by two chairs on the left side of the brick porch. All for looks. Anyone who sat in those chairs went numb from the waist down within minutes.

She'd bought them to suit Will's idea of genteel

welcome. What a way to live. She pushed her key into the lock.

As soon as it turned, she pulled her hand back and stood in front of the doorknob, her fingers spread. Going inside was harder than she'd anticipated.

Will had considered this home, but it had been her compromise. Marriage entailed compromise, but trying to win her husband's love had exhausted her. All the ridiculous arguments she'd backed down from. Why had she tried so hard to be the woman Will wanted?

"Open the door," she said out loud. If she was used to taking orders, she might as well give herself one.

Her heart danced in the back of her throat, but she grabbed the key and opened the door. As if an invisible wall kept her out, she couldn't force her feet to carry her inside. A few flakes of snow, halfhearted remains of the storm, drifted over her shoulder and disappeared before they hit the hardwood floor.

She stared. Nothing had changed. The place looked just as it had three months ago. Wide, polished oak hall, a center table, topped by a Meissen bowl filled with fresh flowers. Someone must have come in since the accident to refresh the roses.

Of course. Will must have hired a cleaner once he'd lost her. He wouldn't want to adjust his habits just because his wife had left.

"Hello?" she called, in case anyone had come today.

No one answered. Isabel took her first step back into the life she'd abandoned. Her former home smelled the same. Her footsteps sounded the same on the overwaxed floors.

Nothing had changed, but she was alien here.

This was no time to let bitterness get the best of her. A lot of work faced her. The house was as clean as Faith's, but different. She and Will had spread his family's heirlooms around their walls and rooms.

Where should she start? She'd leave the kitchen till last since she had to feed herself during this clear-out. She wandered down the wide hall. The gray-blue light of another approaching storm bathed her former home in the dim cold of outside.

Behind her, the doorbell rang.

She jumped. Ben had said he might bring Tony by. She looked at her watch. It couldn't be them already. After playtime in the park, he'd have had to feed the baby.

She'd returned calls from her friends and Will's on the drive over. She still had to answer notes of condolence. She stared at the door, reluctant to face sympathy in person, especially from curious acquaintances who only wanted to know how she and Will had actually finished their relationship.

She plastered a smile on her face and opened the door.

Ben, with Tony perched on his arm, stared at her with a question on his face. "What's wrong?"

She pulled him inside. "I didn't expect you so early."

"But you're glad to see us?"

She ignored his out-of-character doubt as Tony greeted her with such a happy wave he banged his small fist into his father's eye. "My Iz-bell!"

Ben covered his face, and she kissed Tony with a loud smack. "Hey, buddy. You make me feel all better."

"He's not that medicinal for me." Ben teased his son with a quick tickle. "Am I bleeding?"

"Come on. Be a man." Together they laughed, almost like old times. "What did you do with my mom and dad? Are they all right?"

"They're more cheerful after a big breakfast. I left them at my house. I was worried about you."

Isabel frowned. "See—I don't get that. Are you worried because you still care for me, or because you think I'm liable to expose our secret at any moment?"

He ignored her accusation, which made her even more anxious. "You're my family, too. I'm allowed to wonder if you're all right over here," he said. He shut the door and set Tony on the ground. "And you're Tony's aunt." He pulled the child's mittens off. "He kept asking for you, and we decided you might need help. Where do we start?"

"Nowhere yet." She knelt beside Tony and helped him out of his coat as he gabbed in baby talk, complete with pointing. "You remember my house, buddy?"

"My Iz-bell." He grabbed her in a slobbery hug.

He was teething again, but she could stand the moisture. "Tony, remember the pots?" She grinned up at Ben. "Will hated when we played musical pots. Your son's a natural on drums."

"I might hate that, too."

"For you, we'll play plastic. Unless Will got rid of my plastic storage containers. He preferred glass." Taking Tony's hand, she led them to the kitchen. At the door, recognition stopped her dead.

She'd loved this room, its rich woods and the deep farmhouse sink, the island and counters topped in dark brown granite she'd chosen for the warm, pinkish veins that glowed in a reflection of the stove's copper hood.

This room, she'd miss. Clearing the rest of the house would be easy, but how would she say good-bye to this room that had been hers alone?

Sensing Ben behind her, she pretended not to feel sad about leaving the place. "Want coffee?" she asked.

"I'll make it." With the familiarity of long friendship, he opened the appliance garage and took out the coffeepot.

Isabel found the plastic bowls right where she'd left them, on a lazy Susan beside the fridge. She chose a large one, topped it with its lid and offered it, along with a big wooden spoon, to Tony.

Immediately, he began a tune that made Ben turn with exaggerated shock. "That's a mistake."

She laughed but wondered what had changed him from the reserved man she'd hardly recognized into the friend she'd missed. He offered no explanation, though he must have seen her questions. He ran water into the coffeepot while Tony beat out a drum solo.

Isabel squatted beside her nephew. He offered her the spoon, but she shook her head and he went back to playing. Beside his leg, she fingered a gouge in the floor. She'd dropped a casserole that had shattered there. A shard of hard ceramic had chipped out a piece of the golden oak.

"I'll miss this," she said.

"Huh?" Ben cupped his ear. "Can't hear you." He set the carafe on the brewer and hit the power button.

"I'll miss this kitchen. It was mine, maybe the only thing in my life that really belonged to me."

Ben's smile faded. He came around the corner to kneel beside her. "Tony still belongs to you, and I'm not going anywhere."

She tried to smile, but it felt unnatural. "I know. But we both need more than friendship. We're the marrying kind. We need what we thought we had."

"I haven't had a marriage for a long time. I just never admitted it until Faith's note forced me to."

Tony leaned against his dad, beating his bowl with enthusiasm that made Isabel fear for Ben's hand, which held the "drum" still.

She'd missed this man and boy more than Will and Faith. Loving them had been uncomplicated. "What happened between you and Faith?" She sat back on her heels. "Not that I'm sure I want to know what made her go after Will."

He stood and walked Tony toward the hall. "Where do you want to start packing?"

"Wait—I'm sorry. I wasn't blaming you."

"It's okay. I blame you sometimes, too. It's easier than putting the blame with Faith and Will, where it belongs. They can't ever tell us why they betrayed us." He hugged her briefly, surprising her. "Forget it, and I'll tell you the truth. Faith and I grew indifferent. I don't know how it happened or why, and she insisted nothing was wrong—nothing had changed. So I finally stopped fighting."

"A man ought to fight for his marriage."

Ben stopped in midstride outside Will's study. "What about a woman? Did you fight?"

"I kept trying to make Will believe I wanted to be with him. Until he told me about Faith." She felt her skin grow warm. "He convinced me I was the one pushing him away. And I had once, so I felt guilty."

"You sound as if you're used to it. I've known for four days and I can't stop wondering who else is lying to me."

"My husband and my sister. You think you ever get used to it?"

He leaned on the door frame, looking around

Will's study. "Maybe not," he said. "Sorry I put it that way. You've started cleaning in here?"

"No." She stood. Tony slumped over his bowl-drum, listening to different pitches as he hit in various spots. She moved around Ben to eye the papers that littered Will's desk. "He was never this messy. Do you think someone else has been here?"

"I don't know. Check it out. See if you recognize anything he might have been working on."

"I doubt there's anything left in here from three months ago." She studied the desk without touching anything. "I get it," she said. "This bears all the signs of Will's last-minute preparations for a trip."

"Oh." He stood back. "I wonder where they were going."

"Faith didn't tell you?"

"She had no reason. She considered my part in Tony's life over."

Isabel put her hand on his arm to comfort him. He didn't move and he didn't speak, but his doubts came back full force and obvious. She didn't like being the object of Ben's mistrust.

Nervously, she pushed Will's desk chair in. Her former husband's scent was still in the air. His favorite books lay open on the table in front of a sumptuous leather couch that had always felt cold as death to her. "I can't stay in here."

"Why don't we start in the dining room?" Ben's relief matched hers. "You can sort china, and I'll box it up." He prompted his son to stand again, but then let Tony sit in front of the dining room's doorway. "As long as he's pounding that bowl, we'll know where he is. Do you have boxes?"

"In storage above the garage. I should have enough for today. I'll order more."

"You could hire someone to do this."

"I would, but I promised Leah I'd return anything she gave us, as well as Will's things."

"You were married seven years. Now, she wants her gifts back?"

"I don't want anything that reminds me of Will."

His gaze flickered as he glanced toward Tony.

"He doesn't remind me of Will. He's yours."

Ben leveled her with a doubtful glance.

"All right, then. I don't mean him," she said. "You must know that."

"I wasn't thinking of Tony."

"You see what I'm thinking before it's in my head, but I can't read you at all now."

"You just think there's more than I'm telling you."

"Do I?" She wasn't wrong, either.

"You read too much into my wanting Tony to have someone familiar nearby. I know you're leaving after you finish the house."

"What if I move to Pennsylvania to be near my mom and dad?"

"And Leah?" A haunted look shadowed his eyes. "That's your plan?"

She shook her head. It had been a test. "For now, I want to live on my own." Tony began to sing along to his improvised solo, and they both glanced at him. "But I may want to be close to family someday." She tried to imagine the future but saw only gray haze. "When I have children."

"What I'd give to sound so relaxed about having children."

"You can. I'm not telling." She opened the sideboard that towered over the room. The shelves on the closest end held a china service Leah had received from her mother-in-law on the day of her own wedding. Isabel began taking it out.

"How badly do you want kids, Isabel?"

"Not enough to try to take yours."

She lifted her head to find him studying her like one of his experiments. "I'd like to believe you," he said.

"Choose to. You can trust me."

"I did."

Isabel nodded with sarcasm like his. How was she supposed to convince him? Part of her wished with all her heart that she'd told him the truth three months ago. "How was I supposed to tell my best friend he didn't have a son?" She brought more china to the table. "Besides, Faith and Will might have taken Tony away for good as soon as I spoke up."

"Rationalize the best way you can."

His harshness took her breath away, but she refused to let him see. He left, presumably to find the boxes.

She stacked Leah's dishes on the table, with no qualm or regret. She'd loved them at first for the sense of continuity they'd given her. She'd imagined giving them to her own Barker daughter.

Her silly ideas made her sad now. Will couldn't explain why he'd so quickly tired of her but kept her on. She hadn't held a gun to his head to make him propose.

And he wasn't about to rob her of happiness or the daughter or son she'd yearned for. The trick was learning to believe that she'd love someone enough to marry again and have children of her own. Will might have burned her, but his actions wouldn't make her choose a life alone.

"Here we are." Ben came back, stepping over Tony's legs. "I found some newspapers and tossed them in the boxes."

"Newspapers? I always recycled them."

"Will didn't. There are at least three months' worth out there."

He set a couple of stacked boxes on the floor. Isabel opened the top flaps and drew back. Musty newspaper and cardboard odors rose in the room. "They should be okay for dishes, but I hope the drapes don't end up smelling like this. I'm not replacing a damn thing before I sell."

"Careful." With a warning nod in Tony's direction, he reminded her children repeated every "bad" word. "In case Ringo Starr hears you."

"Sorry." She'd already been alone long enough to forget the basics around a boy learning to talk. "Ben?"

"Hmm?" He tossed the dustiest pages of a newspaper into a corner of the parquet floor.

"Can we still ask each other personal questions?"

"You can ask. I don't know that I'll answer."

"What did you mean when you said you had problems before Faith left you her note?"

"Nobody comes to the end of a marriage without warning." He glanced at her in surprise as he pushed the newspaper her way along the table. "Unless you and Will did?"

"He had an affair before we'd been married a year." She stared at the blue pattern on Leah's dishes. "Did you know?"

"Are you kidding? He knew how much I care about you. He wouldn't have told me."

"I don't even know who the woman was." Like Ray, she'd been afraid she'd have to hate someone she knew. She'd been lucky that first time, not having to find out. "We promised to start over, and I tried, but if I'm honest, I'll admit now I never felt exactly the same. When he was late, or gone on business trips, there were moments when I wondered if he was with someone else."

"But you never suspected Faith."

"No, but I noticed the way they looked at each other. I was a little annoyed that they seemed to share private jokes, but I thought they were about me." Isabel concentrated on wrapping a plate with the yellowing newspaper. "Those last few months were tense. We argued more and more about having children, because he didn't want any. Maybe deep down I thought a child would make me commit the way I had at first."

"Did you accuse him of cheating?"

"I asked suspicious questions once or twice, but I always hoped I was wrong." She set the first plate in one of the boxes. "I thought I was supposed to be questioning you."

He peeled another top sheet off a section and pushed the rest to her. "Faith thought I worked too much." He looked at Tony, who'd crawled to the runner in the hall and begun to bang on the rug between smacks on his homemade drum. "I worked longer hours after I started to dread coming home."

"Dread?" Isabel wrapped a salad plate. "Faith never told me."

"I'm guessing Will heard about it." He shrugged as if the thought didn't hurt either of them and then he reached for a salad bowl. "She said she wanted more, that she was bored, alone with Tony all day, no one to talk to. Even you had volunteer work."

"Even I," Isabel said. "As if I was a kindred bored spirit."

"Weren't you?"

"My best times were playing with Tony and Faith. But I kept busy. You know how volunteer committees operate. The wives of the really important men are in charge. I was a gofer—which Will never understood."

"Neither did Faith. She refused to be anyone's lackey, as she put it, and she didn't want to leave Tony long enough to take what she called a 'real' job."

"She said that?"

"She had a degree. I suggested work might keep her from being so bored."

"Why do guys always try to solve your problems with advice?" He looked mystified, as if he'd done his best. It wasn't his fault advice was rarely what a woman wanted from her husband. "Did she tell you what was wrong?"

"Never. More than a year ago, I realized she'd withdrawn, but she insisted she only wanted Tony and his dad." His voice broke. "I couldn't bring her back, and I never expected Tony's dad was my friend."

His voice, dripping in pain, froze Isabel. She clutched a plate in one hand and crumpled a piece of newspaper in the other. Her sister had been cruel.

"Her problem was with me," Ben said. "If I'd been the man she needed, she wouldn't have turned to Will for more."

"I'm speechless." She couldn't look at him. "First, we're on shaky ground because I don't want to know more bad stuff about my sister or my lousy husband. Second, I don't think we should blame ourselves because neither one of them was honest or honorable."

"Will finally told you."

"Because I gave him an ultimatum." Had she brought down her marriage with an emotional challenge? "I said I wanted a baby or it was time to move on."

His surprise startled her. "Did you mean that?"

"I don't enjoy making myself sound manipulative, but I was pretty desperate." She swathed another plate in paper. "You can see why I'm cured of lying or game-playing." She gave him a look that was pure warning. Then she looked at Tony, happily beating the daylights out of her rug.

"He's my priority," Ben said. "All I care about is keeping him."

She didn't blame him, but she didn't know him, either. Isabel had seen him as her friend and Faith's husband. As she looked at him now, he was a large, tough man with dark hair that seemed to erupt from his head in curls. His eyes, dark blue and turbulent, made him seem dangerous.

He folded newspaper around a bowl, his fingers wide and more than capable. Long fingers, lightly veined. Sparse hair on his forearms.

Isabel's heart began a beat that kept up with Tony's recital. She breathed in a scent that wasn't newspaper or box or herself or the house.

Spice and musk and male.

Ben.

She hid a quickened breath. Had she stepped on shaky ground? She might be dancing on the edge of a cliff.

"SIDE, DAD." Tony pointed at the door with his big spoon. "Side, *pease.*"

"You should take him out," Isabel said with dubious enthusiasm. "He's been a patient guy."

Ben's neck muscles relaxed. After an hour, she'd finally spoken. He still didn't know how he'd silenced her. Maybe she needed a break from him and his son.

He was an honest man. Isabel loved spending time with Tony. He was the one who made her uncomfortable.

"We'll check your mail for you," he said. "Without the stroller, that's about as far as Tony can make it." Her mail was delivered to a brick box that contained locked slots for everyone on her street. Set like a stanchion at the far end of the road that curved into her driveway, it was a long walk for a small boy.

"Cool." Isabel was too eager to see them go. "Let me get you the key."

While he helped Tony back into his coat and mittens, Isabel went for her bag. She came back with it, and her search turned up the mailbox key. She handed it to Tony, but he immediately lifted it for a taste, and she had to take it back. "Sorry." Her self-conscious smile made her look more vulnerable than she'd wish. "I forgot."

"Everything goes in the mouth first." He said it by rote. Fathers always said that, but the thought troubling him was how much he'd like to thumb a smudge of dust off her cheekbone.

He'd been lonely for so long, unsure why his wife no longer loved him. And now he'd tricked Isabel into staying in his home so he would know the second she decided to tell her parents the truth about his son. Instead of respecting her and feeling sorry for treating her like an adversary, his loneliness had given him inappropriate feelings for her.

Isabel turned back to the sideboard to move the last of the china to the table. "I'll order more boxes while you're gone." She paused to pull Tony against her leg. "Not that I assume you guys are always going to help me. Mom and Dad won't be willing to let this little one out of their sight for long."

Tony gave her a big smooch and she kissed his cheek with all the noise she could muster.

"Spending more time with him might help your mom," Ben said.

Isabel stopped midway between the sideboard and the table. "You're a good man."

"Huh?" Guilt made him sweat. Was it such a

bad thing, always fearing she'd give away his worst secret?

She set her dishes on the table and then touched his forearm. He felt her hand as he never had before. The weight and the warmth and his uncomfortable awareness of it.

"You could do what Faith and Will tried to do. Run away. I'm the only person who knows enough to stop you, but you talked me into staying. You may not want my mother and father to know about Will's real connection to Tony, but you understand that they need their grandson and he needs them."

"That's a sweet speech, but I feel obliged to point out I'm trying to act normal. Your parents would guess something was up if I disappeared."

She moved as if he'd hurt her. For that, he was sorry. She'd been upset enough, but Tony came first with him, and she shouldn't talk herself into believing anything else.

"Come on, buddy." He swung his son into his arms. "Let's go outside and get mail."

The cold worked wonders. He could almost forget Isabel and the conflicting emotions she caused him. Tony had so many things to investigate, Ben had to trot to keep up. They ran to the end of Isabel's driveway, stopping so Tony could sniff the frozen plants.

"Mmm," he said over and over. Then he pointed for his dad to have a sniff, too.

They didn't smell like a thing, but Ben said "Mmm," too. Then he caught his son's hand and they rounded the fence at the end of the driveway.

Tony tried to lope down the sidewalk, but Ben held him to a pace that kept him from darting into the light traffic. At one house, Tony leaned against the fence. "Woof," he shouted with toddler exuberance. "Woof!"

A dog that couldn't be as big as Tony yapped in response from the other side. Tony doubled over with laughter and woofed again, poking at his hood to push it off his face.

Ben scooped him up. "Want to see the doggy?" He held his son above the fence, and the dog barked like crazy. Tony answered with shrill barks of his own until Ben pulled him back. "We'd better get out of here before the doggy's owner looks for us."

They hurried down the sidewalk until Tony stopped again to peer through a closed wrought-iron gate, yelling "Kit-cat."

Ben stared down at his son. "I don't see a kitty, bud."

"Kit-cat," his boy said again, fully expecting one to materialize.

"Tony, I'm so glad to see you."

The woman's voice startled Ben. He turned as a tall, gray-eyed, steel-haired woman crossed the street from her own driveway.

"Hello." She held out her hand. "You must be

Tony's dad. I was so sorry to hear about your wife and Mr. Barker."

"Thank you," Ben said. "You know my son?"

"I saw him with Faith all the time." She offered Tony a lollipop from her pocket. "Oh, do you mind? Faith always let me give them to him."

"That's fine." A slow burn started in his gut. While he'd been at work, Faith had spent time here—with Will—who'd clearly changed his business hours to suit her. "I'm Ben."

"Marie." She introduced herself. "Tony and I are old friends. He and Faith helped me trim my roses this year. I know she was a great comfort to Mr. Barker after he and his wife split."

"We were all friends." Ben didn't want to hear any more. He suddenly realized that visiting the plants, the dog, even the kit-cat had become Tony's habit when he and Faith had come to Isabel's—Will's—house. He should have assumed Faith would have been coming here while he worked.

"I'll miss your beautiful wife." Marie took his hand again. "As I've missed Isabel. You tell her to stop by before she leaves again. I assume you've come with her?"

He nodded. The woman pounded his shoulder as if she were a coach and he were a failing member of her team.

"You'll see, Ben. Life will brighten up again if you give yourself time to heal."

He tried to smile, but his mouth only twitched. A man who'd run headfirst into a brick wall of betrayal appreciated the thought, but could have done without the platitude.

Tony tucked the woman's lolly into his coat pocket, his hands moving slowly because of his thick mittens. Faith must have trained him to save them for later, after he wasn't running outside.

He took off down the sidewalk on short legs that nevertheless took him swiftly away from his father. "See you later, Marie." Ben hurried after his child.

Tony directed Ben in the proper procedure for checking Isabel's mail. Ben opened the metal box and Tony tugged the pile of letters and magazines out. He dropped half the letters and then he helped Ben pick them up. At last they headed back, no stops this time, to deliver the mail.

All the while, Ben felt as if there were holes in him. Isabel had said he didn't sound like himself. He wasn't acting like himself, either. He nodded at Tony's jabbering and smiled when his son required it, but memories of Faith kicked him in the head. And his strange reaction to Isabel only added to the bruises.

She'd been his friend. Nothing more. He wasn't a man who'd ever cheated on his wife. He'd never lied to Faith. He'd loved her once, respected her, believed she and Tony were his future.

By the time he and Tony reached Isabel's door, he

was fighting angry tears no man would let himself cry.

"Weel?" Tony asked for his uncle as Ben turned the doorknob.

Ben cringed. Naturally, Tony missed Will, but the other man's name on his son's lips terrified Ben. At any moment, if Isabel chose her parents over him, Amelia and George could tear Tony out of his arms, and he might have no recourse.

"Sorry, buddy." Ben lifted him as he opened the door and then shut it and turned the lock. "Will's not here."

"Mom?" Isabel came out of the dining room, her cell phone to her ear. "You're making a brisket?" She smiled at Tony but looked mystified. "You only ate breakfast a couple of hours ago." Her mother's grief-fueled vitality confused her. "What?" Her surprise stopped him. "A letter came," she said, her voice fading. "From Will? No, don't open it. I don't want to hear—"

The phone hit the floor.

CHAPTER FIVE

BEN SET TONY DOWN and then hurried to Isabel's side. She leaned into him, instinct making them close again. He'd never seen her willingly lean on anyone. Not even Will.

"My mom." She pointed her finger at the floor. She was shaking head to toe. He held on while he picked up the phone.

"Amelia?" he said.

"Ben, what's wrong with Isabel?" Amelia sounded terrified.

"Nothing," he said. "She dropped the phone."

Isabel covered the phone's speaker. "I gave my office your address because I wasn't sure I'd be able to get inside this house."

"But how did Will get the Middleburg address?"

She tugged his arm, impatience in her clenched fingers. "I gave it to him. I expected divorce papers." She said "divorce" matter-of-factly, but her panic was contagious. "We have to stop my mom from reading that letter. He may have said something about Tony."

He searched for his son, who'd returned to the drum.

"Give me the phone, Ben. She'll open it."

"Isabel says to just put the letter in the guest room, Amelia. She'll read it when she gets back."

Isabel waited. Her mother's voice was loud enough to hear. "If you're sure."

"Thanks, Amelia."

"Will you be home soon? Tony loves brisket, doesn't he?"

"I don't know." Faith would have known. She might have been right about his inattention. But he'd learn everything about his boy from now on. "I'll bring him right now." He had to make sure she didn't open that letter.

Isabel squeezed his arm again. She mouthed the word *thanks*. Then she brushed her jeans and sweater, dragging her composure back on like clothing. He held out the phone, but she shook her head.

Tony dropped his drum, but advanced upon the dining room, with his big spoon at the ready. "We'll be on our way soon, Amelia."

"Okay."

He turned the phone off. Isabel rubbed her sleeve, but she no longer looked as grateful. "Sorry," she said. "I won't fall apart again."

"Forget it. I'll be right back. Tony's probably on the verge of playing with a priceless gravy boat."

"He can break it all. Why would Will send me a letter? I already knew too much about him and Faith."

"Maybe it is the divorce papers."

She lifted her eyebrows. "That's probably it. Funny how much I don't want to see them."

"Don't assume, Isabel. Will's surprised us before." Torn between her and his son, he had only one choice. "Let me get Tony."

He raced into the dining room and caught his boy just as Tony was reaching for one of the cardboard boxes. "Hold on there."

Tony complained and reached again, but Ben returned him to the hall where his drum was, just as Isabel was pushing both hands into the small of her back.

Ben wished he could help her, but one thing he'd already learned—they had to do their grieving and surviving alone. He moved all the boxes to safer heights in the dining room.

Isabel had moved to the door when he came back. "You should go," she said. "Mom will wonder what's taking so long."

"I don't like leaving you."

"I dressed Tony in his coat and hat."

"Why are you angry, Isabel? I didn't mean to take over. I just…"

"Thought I needed help." Her head came up. She clenched her fists. "I want you to go, and I'll handle my own problems from now on."

"We're in this together, helping each other."

"You can't help me get over Will, and I can't help

you with your feelings for Faith." She glanced at Tony as if she'd rather he didn't hear. "That letter is probably one more lie—nothing to lose sleep over."

What kind of idiot had Will been to throw away such a woman? Fierce, loyal, strong. Qualities neither Faith nor Will had valued.

Ben stared at Isabel and she stared back, loneliness passing between them on a river of unspoken hurt.

Tony began to cry. "Mommy?"

His broken entreaty hurt more than anything so far. Ben lifted his child, who needed him more than any woman would again. Tucking Tony's head beneath his chin, Ben reached for the door. "Call if you need anything. Otherwise, we'll see you at home later."

She nodded. This was the one moment they should help each other.

"What do you want now, Isabel?"

She obviously wanted him to go. "I don't know." She straightened Tony's mitten. "I don't like feeling you and I have changed toward each other."

"It was that phone call. You're not used to having someone protect you."

"I don't need protection."

She dropped her hands to her sides, unnaturally stiff. He searched himself for compassion. Her pain went as deep as his. "You're my friend," he said, "like it or not. Our lives are tangled up together."

For the first time, comforting her mattered more than keeping her from telling her parents the truth about Tony.

ISABEL LOST all interest in clearing the house after Ben and Tony left. She closed the door behind them and slid to the floor. She didn't know how long she sat there, back to the wall.

Will had written a letter. Or sent her a letter some attorney might have written for him. Who knew what it meant or why the idea of a divorce should still hurt. She'd fallen out of love with Will—maybe even as far back as that first affair. But she'd promised him a second chance and she'd tried as hard as she could.

Not hard enough or he wouldn't have turned to her sister.

Finally the arguments in her head subsided enough to let in a little silence. She stood up and found her purse and coat. Late afternoon was trying to turn into dusk as she followed slow traffic through the snow, back to Ben's.

Her father greeted her at the door with flour dotting the edge of his glasses. Good smells swam around him—fresh bread and the rich tang of a fulsome soup. Her mom had taught Faith how to make a home, and this home reflected her mom's care.

"Hi," Isabel said. "I thought we were having brisket."

"It burned."

"I'm stunned."

Her dad pulled her inside and hugged her before he let her go. "Imagine how your mom felt. I don't think she's had a failure like this since she burned the bottom out of the giblet pan our first Thanksgiving."

Isabel had heard that story a few times—when her dad felt her mom needed to be pulled back from the ego-boosting edge of perfection. "Thanks for the laugh."

"For once, your mom wouldn't mind me bringing it up. We had the windows open all afternoon."

She glanced at her watch. She'd sat on that floor for a hell of a long time.

"Are you okay, honey?"

She nodded but hugged him again. "You're better tonight."

"I've had plenty to do."

So work was key? She'd remember that next time she pined against a wall. "Where are Ben and Tony?"

"Ben's persuading Tony to use his high chair. Give me your coat." He pulled it off her. "You're trembling. Is it that cold outside?"

Isabel pulled herself together. "It's snowing again. I'd better go read that letter."

"Are you worried about something Will might have said?" He put his fingers beneath her chin. "Why are you frightened?"

"No reason." She tried to brazen it out, but her father didn't believe her. "I dread hearing from him

after all this time. And I can't talk to him about whatever he's said." A bad taste in her mouth cut her off.
What a lie. If Will had wanted talk, he'd have called
her. He'd wanted his say and no hint of an argument
from her.

She hoped Faith had enjoyed being his grown-up
doll more than she had.

"I'm going upstairs."

"Wait." Her father stopped her. "How long do you
plan to stay here?"

"I don't know." Was he suspicious? "Until I
finish the house. I can't really afford a hotel right
now."

"No. Your mother and I thought we'd go home.
We can come back if Tony or Ben needs us."

"I'm sure Tony is better off, having you so close."

"He dragged your mother out for a turn around the
park while the brisket smell cleared out of the
house." He smiled reflectively. "That walk did her
good."

"Don't go yet, Dad."

"Huh?"

She wasn't used to asking for favors. She'd always been the responsible daughter, the one who
took life on the chin. Faith had needed their help—
to pay school loans and credit-card bills and the occasional car payment before she'd married Ben.
They'd expected their more delicate daughter to
need their help.

Surprising herself as much as her dad, Isabel threw her arms around him and hung on. "I need you. Can't you stay a few more days? There's plenty of room for you and Mom here."

"No. Your mom's better during the day, but at night, with nothing to do except look at the ceiling and remember Faith in this house, she might slip back." He hugged her. "But I have this friend. He spends winters in Florida and he might lend me his condo in D.C."

"Could you call him tonight?" She didn't want to be left alone with her disillusionment over Will, her anger with Faith and her confusion about Ben.

She and her parents had long ago adopted a live-and-let-live policy that kept them respectful of one another's privacy. Tonight she needed more.

"I'll talk to your mother on the way back to the hotel."

"Thanks, Dad. I'm going up to change and read that letter. Tell Mom I'll be down as soon as I clean up a little. I feel like a dust ball."

"Take your time." He took her hand as she turned to the stairs. "And yell if you need me."

She laughed with relief. Her father understood. His empathy strengthened her. She wasn't really the weak woman who'd collapsed in Ben's arms.

In her room, the letter lay on a dresser, a large white envelope with Ben's address stickered over her business address in Middleburg.

What else could Will have hidden from her? She breathed deep to keep from choking.

Turning her back on the letter, she made up her bed. And then she unpacked the clothes and toiletries she'd left in her bag.

At last she couldn't find another task to put between her and opening the letter. She picked it up and sat in a straight-backed chair. Outside, darkness shaded the window. Downstairs, Tony laughed with the sheer joy only a child knows. Ben's deep voice echoed his son's.

Ben and Tony. A normal man and boy in a world where she felt increasingly like a stranger. She loved them. They loved her. Ben needed her here for some reason she didn't understand yet, but he'd never hurt her. Why not throw the letter away and go downstairs?

Why not?

Because she was no longer the weak-kneed puddle of compliance that Will Barker had bent to suit his plans. She jerked the envelope open so fast it tore.

A single page fluttered to the floor. She picked it up, recognizing Will's writing with a slight pang.

Dear Isabel, I'm sorry, but Faith and I are leaving together, and we're taking our son. Everyone will know the truth about us and about Tony by the time you read this. I wanted to

warn you that Faith has persuaded me to take
it all out in the open.

She looked up, barely seeing the pale green walls.
He'd needed convincing? Isabel's mouth went dry
with anger. Though he'd cheated on her and tried
to ruin Ben's life, she felt her deepest contempt because he'd had to be convinced to acknowledge
Tony.

You won't be that surprised that we're leaving.
You know you never forgave me for that first
slip. I needed you to look at me again with
complete love. Instead you became repressed.
I was so lonely I turned to Faith to find ways
to win you back. She was unhappy, too, bored
with Ben's ambitions and his refusal to give her
the good time and the interesting company she
and I both enjoy.

Those dinner parties that had been sheer hell and
boredom for her. But Faith had treated each one like
a gala celebration.

We tried to say no to our feelings, but Faith and
I are soul mates as you and I couldn't be. If
you'd fallen in love as I have, I would never
have tried to hold you. Please understand and
know that in my own way I loved you once.

She dropped the letter, laughing without joy. Almost immediately, a knock rattled the door. Ben must have been standing there.

She breathed deep, tried to stop laughing.

Without knocking again, Ben burst inside. He stumbled, stopping just before he landed on the bed.

Isabel laughed harder.

"I thought you'd lock it," he said.

She put her hands over her mouth until she could stop. Her face felt wet. She must be crying.

"Your dad said you came up to read this." He picked up the letter. "I would have come with you. You should have waited."

"Take a look."

"No." He held it out. "I came to make sure you were all right, but I don't want to know anything else."

"You'll get a laugh, too."

"I doubt it." But he turned the letter faceup. It was irresistible torture.

"No," she said, trying to take it back. "It's mean, and everything he said was a lie." Ben didn't need Will's side of it. He hadn't had three months to start healing.

Ben read anyway, but he didn't laugh. When he finished, he dropped it on the floor, ground it beneath his heel and wrapped his arms around her.

"Twisted bastard."

Isabel laughed again. She caught his shirt in both

hands. His heart wasn't bleeding through it. "They were Romeo and Juliet."

"And we were stooges, but we're still here and we're going to survive. Let him go, Isabel."

"Why did I try so hard? 'In my own way I loved you once.' If I'm lucky, I'll live the rest of my life without love like his."

"Will loved himself."

"And Faith." She stared at the crumpled paper. "I think they were together for longer than three years."

"We'll never know. Will lied to justify an affair, and he obviously wants you to congratulate him for his brief self-control."

"I can understand—just barely—not being able to control their feelings, but didn't either of them ever hear of divorce?"

"Will avoided public scandal. It wasn't good for his company, but more than that—he didn't believe he could do anything wrong. They were afraid and ashamed, and Will wasn't man enough to admit your problems were his fault, too."

"Too?" She pulled away and tugged down the hem of her sweater. "You don't believe what he said about me being repressed?"

Light glinted from Ben's eyes for the first time since she'd been back. "I'm glad it pissed you off," he said.

She hated to encourage him with a smile. "Why don't you go downstairs? I'm going to wash my face and then I plan to eat until I can't move."

He went without argument. Isabel tucked the letter into an inner pocket in her suitcase. Then she splashed her face with cold water until she looked less as if she'd been crying. Then she hurried to the kitchen where her family had gathered at the table. "Everything looks great, Mom. Shiny and bright."

Her dad stood. "Your mother cleaned a bit this afternoon. She made me help her."

"Good going, Mom."

"If he's not careful, we may start on the closets." Her mother smiled, but it was obviously an effort. Though grief and exhaustion strained her face, she still tried to be cheerful.

Tony beat his spoon against his bowl. "Iz-bell," he said, as happy as if she were a Christmas present.

She searched for a non-soupy patch of skin to kiss. "Hey, you—heart of my heart." She kissed, tasted and then grinned at her mother. "I love corn chowder."

"I'm sorry about the brisket, but I thought this made a nice substitute. We can all use comfort food."

Isabel sat down. "I feel like a slacker, getting here in time to eat but not to help."

"You already have a big job, and I was glad to tidy up and make dinner." Her mother offered Ben her strange, sad warmth. "The sooner this house feels like a home again, the better for our men."

"I appreciate the way the house looks, and dinner is delicious." Ben scooped a spoonful of soup and offered it to his son. "But you don't have to take care of us, Amelia. Try to enjoy playing with Tony."

"Your mom and Tony went to the park this afternoon," Isabel's father said as if he hadn't told her before. "They played on the slide and climbed the jungle gym," he said.

"I held Tony up to the bars. He grabbed and then dangled." Her mom tried another smile. "Your father's trying to advise you not to worry about me. I'll be back to normal soon."

"Normal's a concept none of us is familiar with right now."

"What did Will's letter say?" Amelia asked.

Accidentally, Isabel looked at Ben before an answer came into her head. "He wanted to let me know how the business was going." He'd hardly ever shared business news with her during seven years of marriage. She hoped she'd been too *repressed* to complain about it to her mother.

Apparently so. Her mom nodded, and her dad joined in. Isabel took advantage of the opening to spew a step-by-step report of all she'd done at her own house. While relating every move she'd made, she helped Ben feed Tony so he could take the occasional bite himself.

"This is delicious, Mom. I was starving."

"Were you, honey?" Her appetite pleased her mother. "I thought solid and warm." She passed a plate of jalapeño cheese bread. "And what's a carbohydrate or two among family?"

After dinner, Isabel volunteered to clean the kitchen. Ben swept Tony off for a bath—trailing bits of corn behind him. She heard him speaking in the family room. The low rumble of his voice drew her to the open kitchen doorway.

"Come help us, Amelia. Tony loves company at bath time."

"You think? George, did you want to leave anytime soon?"

"We're not under curfew. You go ahead."

Before they could catch her eavesdropping, Isabel busied herself with dishes, scrubbing a little harder than she needed to, giving in to adrenaline rather than reverencing Faith's china.

Ben might be trying to turn himself into a cruel, distrustful man, but inside, his compassionate heart still beat. He'd invited her mom to help with Tony because he knew how much she needed a connection to her grandson.

But Isabel thought back to last night. Didn't Ben realize Tony could remind her mother to live again?

Once again caught between her best friend and her parents, Isabel launched an attack on the cluttered counters. She could become everyone's enemy in the time it took to put the truth about Faith and Will into words.

Her parents wouldn't understand why she hadn't told them. Ben would cut her out of his and Tony's life if she did. Unless her parents took the baby from him.

And could she bear that? Hadn't Ben lost enough because of her family?

The black granite counters gleamed under Isabel's scrubbing. She tucked every superfluous appliance away, dried the dishes and returned them to their cabinets.

Water ran overhead, and laughter rang out. Isabel smiled, imagining her mother wrestling Tony into the tub. No one ever gave him enough floaty toys. Plus, he loved to write on the tub with crayon soap. The tub and himself and any unsuspecting soul foolhardy enough to come near him.

Finally Isabel threw the damp dish towels down the laundry chute and loaded the coffeemaker with ground beans and water for the morning.

All the while she prayed her parents would leave and Ben would stay immersed in the cycle of lullabies Tony demanded each night. A clear path up the stairs to her room would solve her most immediate problems. She knew too much and she didn't want to talk to anyone.

After the din of splashing and laughter finally died down, she crept to the family room. Her father set his paper in his lap.

"Tired?" he asked.

"Exhausted. I'm going to bed."

"Are you okay? Is it too hard going into your old house?"

Difficult because she'd lost everything marriage brought a couple—intimacy, trust, happiness. But her father couldn't know she'd barely had those things with Will.

"It's not fun, but I have to sell the place, and Leah wants her belongings back. I can't blame her. They remind her of Will and her husband."

"You should set them aside and make her come get them."

"I'd rather handle it myself." She smiled without seeing anything funny in the image of Leah whirling like the Tasmanian devil through the house, collecting goods along the way. "Night." She kissed his papery cheek. "I love you, Dad."

"You know how much your mother and I love you. We're distracted right now because of Faith, but don't feel we loved her more."

That might be true for him. Faith had definitely been her mother's favorite. Isabel believed she'd learned to take second place in stride, but sometimes she wondered if she was keeping the secret in some unconscious act of revenge.

Like a cat burglar, she hurried to her room. As she passed the nursery, peals of her mother's laughter all but pinned her to the wall. She'd heard that sound so many times in her teenage years, reminding her she and her mom didn't have the ease her mother and Faith had shared.

"Ben, be careful," she said in a whisper.

BEN WOKE before light was more than a blue shadow between the drapes at his window. He'd wrestled with dreams of chasing Faith, fighting Will, to take back his son.

And always, Isabel stood to the side in nightmare indifference, refusing to act for him but making no move against him. He suspected more than exhaustion had made her turn in early last night.

She'd been glad to see him and Tony leave her house yesterday and then she'd sent him downstairs ahead of her after they'd read the letter. He'd assumed she wanted to compose herself, but something more might be driving her.

He tried to remember Will's letter, but all he'd taken from it was the fact that his so-called best friend hadn't truly wanted Tony, and that Will and Faith had blamed him and Isabel for everything that had gone wrong.

Lies. He'd take his fair share of blame, but no man forced his wife to sleep with her sister's husband.

Lies? Ben pushed back his bedding. Isabel's one refrain since she'd come back had been a refusal to live with lies. She might be right about the inevitability of his situation. If her mother had read that letter yesterday, the truth about Tony would have come out.

He rubbed cold sweat off his forehead and crossed the room to open his door. Isabel's was closed still.

Relief swamped him. Uneasily, he admitted that

she might not have his worst interests at heart. She was trying to help him, though she obviously felt uncomfortable not telling her parents the truth.

He had to make sure she wasn't changing her mind.

He glanced at Tony's door and then looked back at the clock in his room. Last night, in the middle of Tony's enthusiastic bath, Amelia had suggested she and George might take him downtown to the Smithsonian. He'd agreed but half expected she'd call to cancel when the apathy of grief took over again this morning. But he needed to talk to Isabel. With any luck Amelia would still want time with her grandson more than she'd want to be alone with her pain and her husband.

For a second, he wondered what it would be like to depend on another human being when you'd lost everything else that mattered, but he had no time to feel sorrier for himself. He showered and went downstairs to start Tony's breakfast. After the Deavers showed up and then left with Tony, he'd face Isabel with his doubts.

She'd get the look that told him he was hounding her. She'd remind him they were only putting off the inevitable, but he was willing to take the chance that he could keep his son's birth father a secret for the next sixteen-and-a-half years.

ISABEL OUTFOXED him. While he was making Tony's cereal, he heard a faint sound that turned out to be the front door opening and then closing.

He dialed her cell phone number. She didn't answer. That stung.

He stirred warm milk into the cereal until it formed the pastelike consistency Tony liked. His hand shook.

"Dad-dee!" Tony's morning bellow.

"Coming, son." He ran up the stairs to fly his boy out of the crib. They ate breakfast and finished dressing as the Deavers rang the bell. With Tony perched on one arm, Ben opened the door. George reached for his grandson. Amelia tucked an orange scarf into her beige overcoat. The first time she hadn't worn black.

"Hey." He let Tony go to George.

"Hello, my bunny." Amelia kissed the baby's nose. "Shall we see some of those rocks you like so much?"

"Rocks," Tony said with a couple of extra *r*'s. He opened his hand and closed it, reaching for the stairs. "Iz-bell?"

"Where is Isabel today?" Amelia glanced over Ben's shoulder. "Still asleep?"

"I think she already left to work on the house." Ben stood aside to let them in. Amelia came inside. George looked surprised. "In fact," Ben said, "I thought I'd help her while you all are downtown. We could make some good progress today."

"Sounds like a great idea," Amelia said. "Tony loves the Natural History museum. By the time we see all of it and have lunch on the Mall, he'll be ready for a long nap."

"Lunch outside in this cold?" With the door open, the wind blew at him with a knife's edge.

"Calm down, Ben. We won't risk our little guy. If it's too cold we'll eat inside one of the museums." George opened the closet door with Tony on his shoulder. "Where's your coat, buddy?"

Tony wriggled around to question Ben. "Iz-bell?" He pointed at the stairs again. "Iz-bell," he said, his small voice raising.

"Not here right now," Ben said. "She'll come back tonight."

"Help me with his coat, Amelia." While she helped George, Ben ran upstairs and packed a bag with extra diapers and juice boxes. He tried to give the Deavers money for Tony's lunch, but they looked at him as if he'd lost his mind. They'd probably fed him a time or two in the days before Ben had become so paranoid about anyone else doing anything for his son.

Distracted because he couldn't get Isabel and the letter out of his head, he put Tony's car seat in the back of George's car. Tony peered over George's shoulder as the older man tried to buckle him in.

"Let me do that, George."

"We're fine," George said. He tickled his grandson and Tony giggled, relaxing in his seat. Ben gripped the door frame, trying to ignore second thoughts about sending his child off with the two people who were most likely to try to take him.

He struggled with his own instincts. Keeping his son away from the Deavers would make them ask why. His laughing son caught and held Ben's gaze. He'd been a loving father. He'd changed diapers and walked him when he was sick, and he'd sung his half of the nightly lullabies.

He'd tried to work out his problems with Faith, thinking a loving husband was a good example to set. He couldn't cut Tony's grandparents out of his life. A boy needed all the love due to him.

Ben walked Amelia to the front passenger seat. She took his hand.

"You don't think something in Will's letter upset Isabel?"

He went blank. "I do," he finally said, though his first impulse was to lie again so she wouldn't worry or ask herself what the letter contained. How the hell did a man keep up with lie after lie? "It was probably the letter itself. She only left Will three months ago. That's hardly time to get over a bad cold, much less a seven-year marriage."

Amelia rested her hand on the car door. "She didn't tell you anything?"

Nothing she'd want him to share. "Trust her, Amelia. She'll talk to you when she's ready." God, he hoped not. He released the door. "You have my cell phone number?"

Amelia teared up. "Faith used to ask me that every time she left Tony with me."

He opened his mouth to ask when Faith had left Tony with Amelia. As far as he knew, she'd only gone to visit her mother to make sure Tony had family time.

Amelia might mean that Faith had left Tony with her while she'd gone out with friends or something equally innocent. He couldn't ask without looking foolish—maybe even suspicious—but he searched his memory for times when Faith and Will had both been out of town. If he could live the past three years over again, he'd start by opening his eyes.

"Time to roll, honey," George said, across the roof.

Amelia smiled at her husband and then hugged Ben before she climbed into her seat. "We'll take good care of Tony."

They were gone before he could unclench his fists. Lucky he'd stayed behind. By now, he'd have been grilling Amelia for dates and times.

He went back inside and cleaned up the breakfast things. After he finished, he took a last look at the sink and the chrome and reflective granite. He'd never made the kitchen shine to Faith's satisfaction.

He threw the dish towel on the counter and turned his back on the room. A few minutes later, he was on his way to Isabel's house. She looked surprised to see him when she answered her door.

"Where's Tony?"

"Your parents took him to the Smithsonian. I'm here to do whatever you need." *And also shadow you until I know whether guilt over keeping your parents in the dark is getting to you.*

Her expression begged him to be honest.

"What's wrong?" he asked.

"The usual. I don't entirely trust you." She stopped with a smile more cynical than he'd ever seen. "Don't look hurt. You know you have ulterior motives for hanging around me."

"And they would be?"

"You know I wouldn't hurt you. Even if I didn't love you and Tony, I'd owe you because I didn't warn you after Will told me about him and Faith." She searched him, head to toe, with a look. "I can't figure out what I have that you want. Something you can't tell me about."

She might just as well have banged his soul with a hammer. Guilt made him wish he was a better man.

"Aren't you holding any grudges, Isabel?"

"Against you? For what?" Her soft smile held sorrow. "Are you still angry with me?"

"No." At least he could be honest about that. "But I'm not over what happened."

"Every time I look at Tony, I'm torn. I should have done something to help you three months ago. Then I wonder if my parents need to know about Will."

"Why?" His heart threatened to stop. And then it seemed to pound so fast he could barely hear over the blood rushing through his veins. "What possible good could knowing do them?"

Isabel locked the door. "I can't see them trying to take him from you, but I wonder how Tony will accept the news if he finds out when he's older. How would you feel if your father and your aunt lied about who you were all your life?"

"He's my son. He's never belonged to any other man."

"You're right about that." She looked angry now. "What kind of man would refuse to acknowledge him?"

Suddenly, he couldn't talk about Tony. He felt the cold grasp of panic when he thought too hard about Faith and Will and their plans.

"Are you still going back to Middleburg after you sell the house?" he asked.

Concern shadowed her eyes, but she let him change the subject. "I need a job, but hiding out in Middleburg doesn't seem like such a smart idea after all. This house isn't right, either, but I've loved living in this area."

"The sale price should give you a start anyplace." He should hope she'd go far away and leave him in greater peace with his son. Instead, he tried to imagine life without Isabel at the end of a short drive, and he didn't care for his sense of loss.

She led him to the living room, half denuded of knickknacks and paintings. The hall echoed without the runner she'd rolled into a wool cylinder. "You sure you want to help?"

"That's why I came."

Her qualms hit him full force. Without facing the truth, they weren't really talking, but it was easier to ignore the argument that could split them up forever.

"All that stuff in the corner gets boxed up for Leah. The new boxes should arrive any minute."

He noted a smaller pile of objects on a side table. Framed photos. Will's diplomas. "What's all this?" He'd be happy to set the stack on fire.

Her reluctance warned him. "They're for Tony." She apologized with a shrug. "Someday, if you think he should have them."

"If I tell him Will was his real father?"

"His birth father. You might change your mind by the time Tony's old enough to know." She waved at the diplomas as if she didn't care about them at all. "Or if you'd honestly prefer it, we can destroy them," she said. "Or send them to Leah. You don't have to decide now."

"You haven't had a child—you can't know how I feel when I contemplate losing him."

Isabel's broken smile reminded him how much she'd wanted a baby of her own. With an index finger, she pushed the top frame farther into the center of the table.

"I threw them in the trash when I started cleaning his office this morning." Lifting her face, she looked naked and young and vulnerable. "Throwing them away made me feel better.

"I'm glad." He pulled her close, and she put her arms around him. Her body, alive, warm, responsive to his affection, gave him comfort though he'd reached for her to ease her suffering.

"But I only felt better for a second," she said, and then laughed, mocking herself. "Maybe more than a few seconds. I thought, what if Ben tells Tony who Will really was to him? Tony will want information."

"I'll never tell him."

"Secrets don't seem to stay kept," she said. "Or you and I wouldn't be dumbfounded that Faith and Will had an eighteen-month-old son."

"We wanted to believe in them. That's half the battle."

"You know what the worst thing is?" She pushed away from him. "Sometimes, when I first wake up and remember everything's changed, I almost— almost—wish I could still believe. Nobody else on earth would have any claim to Tony. You and I might not be perfectly happy, but we'd be muddling along, trying to make the best of our marriages."

He hated to think of Isabel settling for a husband who'd wasted her life the way Will had. "I've been irritated because you seem impervious to what happened."

"I'm determined to win. Faith and Will are not going to change me for the worse."

Ben almost said, "But I might." Forcing her to lie. Putting his own desperate need above her feelings.

"Can I say one more thing?" Sunlight, through a sheer, pale curtain, lightened her hair.

He nodded, because he couldn't speak over sudden awareness that seemed to suffocate him. His palms burned. He saw himself touching her hair, smoothing the lines from her worried frown.

"You don't know yourself as well as I know you," Isabel said. "You're man enough to wait until Tony's older before you get rid of Will's things. You can decide what to do with them after you give up the idea of revenge."

"I have changed." He was trying to tell her who he'd become—he'd hurt even her if his life with Tony depended on it.

"Not that much. You'll love someone else someday, and you'll make room for her in your life and Tony's."

"I'm never going to change my mind about Tony, Isabel. Give up any hopes you have about that."

She shook her head, and light followed the strands of her hair. When she looked at him with such confidence, he almost believed in the future she saw. "We'll both love someone eventually and we'll trust them because that's who you and I are."

His head went back as if she'd slapped him. "Not a chance," came out of his mouth.

Isabel waved both hands dismissively, as if he were talking nonsense. Her wedding rings twinkled on her fingers. She noticed them at the same moment.

She turned her hand over and stared at the rings. Then she pulled them off and opened a drawer on a fragile table beside the couch. She dropped the jewelry in and slammed it shut.

"I'm going to love again. I want children of my own, and I intend to be happy. I'll make myself trust a man if it kills me."

"How do you plan to do all that?"

"I deserve real love and so do you."

"What we deserve and what we get are obviously two different things. Why don't you know that?"

"Don't put any more pictures of Will and Faith in my head." She pressed her fists to her temples, and her sweater outlined her breasts in loving curves. Its hem skimmed the top of her jeans, revealing a hint of hip bone.

His body grew heavy. He turned his back on her. He had no right to think of Isabel like that.

"I'm sorry, Ben." She went on, unaware he'd lost the ability to form words. "I didn't mean to snap at you."

"Don't apologize when you haven't done anything wrong." If he tried to explain, she'd consider him as twisted as Will and Faith. He'd held her— kissed her—maybe a thousand times without ever wanting more. What made today different?

The doorbell rang. He almost leaped across the couch and the console table behind it. "I'll get that."

A man from a packing store had brought more boxes and wrapping paper. Ben helped him carry everything inside.

By the time they were alone again, he'd regained his sense of right and wrong. They worked, shared a delivered pizza, and then worked a few hours longer with no more drama.

Ben tried not to think of the morning's strange revelations. He was a man. Men wanted women. It didn't have to go further than that.

Isabel finally gave up for the day after they'd culled any object Leah had ever given her from every room in the house. He helped her box them, grateful for the physical exertion. Then he called the delivery service to schedule a morning pickup.

"This will cost a fortune," he said as they surveyed the boxes they'd stacked in the entry.

"Worth every penny."

"I could drive you up with them."

"I'm in no mood to see Leah, and this will keep her in Philadelphia while she inventories it to make sure I haven't held anything back." That sounded about right for Leah.

"Legally, this stuff belongs to you."

"Not in my eyes or hers. She made up some story about forcing me to put up with her because I wouldn't believe she wanted to stay in touch." Isa-

bel patted the top of the nearest box. "I believe a mix-
ture of her words and deeds. She might think I'm her
last physical connection with Will, but she wants her
family possessions back, too."

"And you think this woman makes a good grand-
mother for Tony?"

Isabel smoothed tape on the box and looked uncomfortable. "There's a higher morality, you know.
When I put myself in Leah's place, I don't know that
we have a right to keep her last blood relative away
from her." She wrapped her arms around her waist.
"She can be a little crazy and vindictive. I know she
wasn't a picture-perfect mom for Will, but she loved
him—maybe the best she could—and Tony is part of
him, whether you and I like it or not."

Being reminded of Will's actual role in Tony's
birth made him imagine Will and Faith together.
When he added the fear of losing his son, he couldn't
stand it.

But Isabel had nothing to do with Will and Faith's
lies. "I'm sorry," he said. "I keep trying to make you
admit I'm right because I want to feel safe."

"I believe we're doing the right thing, but I'm not
sure we should be doing it."

He took her hand. "I need to know you're on my
side—that we'd both risk anything for Tony."

She shook her head. Her hair brushed her shoulders, releasing a scent uniquely Isabel, woman and
a hint of perfume no chemist had ever formulated.

"Mom and Dad are my family, too, Ben. And Leah has been my mother-in-law. I'm doing what you asked, but I have doubts."

"I don't care about morality. I want my son safe and happy, and I won't give him up."

"The truth is hanging over his head. It could come out because of an illness, if his blood type is incompatible with yours. It could come out if my mother finds a note between Will and Faith where they talk about Tony."

He shuddered. Time for him to search his own home, top to bottom. "Even if you're right, I won't admit that I was not Tony's father."

"I guess that's it." Obviously troubled, she turned toward the kitchen. "I'll get my things, and we can lock up. Put on your coat."

"I have to stop on the way home for groceries and diapers."

He pushed his arms into his coat sleeves, but in his head, he walked down that long hall at Isabel's side. He and his son had spent so much of their lives with her.

He kept telling himself Tony was enough for him. He could lie to the Deavers and Leah about Tony's birth father till doomsday. Hell, he'd lie to the courts if it came to that.

But he couldn't lie to himself. Someday, Isabel would be forced to choose sides, and he didn't want to lose her.

CHAPTER SIX

IN FRONT OF HER, Ben's car peeled away from the curb and started to fishtail. Fear grabbed her by the stomach and gave a shake, but then the ice lost its grip and he straightened out.

She bested an almost physical need to call and warn him not to scare her with his driving when Faith and Will had died that way. She'd scolded him enough for one night.

He had her all confused. She'd felt like such a fool when she'd discovered Faith's and Will's lies, and yet she couldn't imagine how Tony would feel losing Ben, on top of his mother and uncle's death.

Isabel parked in front of Ben's garage and got out, her muscles sore from packing and the tension of worrying and arguing with Ben.

As soon as she shut her car door, she heard Tony shrieking with joy in the backyard. Just the sound of his voice changed everything. His happiness warmed her even in new falling snow. She headed for the gate, drawn by his careening-down-the-slide laugh.

Her father stood guard from behind the slide. Too far away. She hurried toward her nephew.

"Dad, we always help him with the ladder," she said.

"Sorry, honey." Grief still gave him a tendency to look stunned. "I didn't think."

Isabel loved her father, who was wounded but carrying on as best he could.

"Iz-bell!"

"Tony!" She opened her arms and he flew at her. She caught him in midair and then swung him until they faced his grandfather.

Tony wriggled down and then bolted for the slide. George leaned over to help this time, but Tony pushed his hands away as he climbed.

"He knows how," George said.

"Yes, he's much better." She stayed on the lookout, not as sanguine as her dad about his physical prowess. "But he's still small."

"You haven't seen him for the past three months," her father said. "I'm not sure your mom and I have, either."

"None of us could know what would happen, Dad."

"I talked to Faith a few times. She thought you were angry with her."

Nice cover, Faith. "She sided with Will in our problems." That was as close as she could get to the truth. If she said any more, her father might tumble into the whole mystery.

"Why would Faith let you down like that? You were always close. Boys didn't come between you. Other friends never split you up."

Tony ran around the slide, shouting as he clambered up again. Tears, unexpected and hot, stung Isabel's eyes. Love had changed her sister. "Don't worry, Dad. Faith and I disagreed. Let's drop it there."

"I'd rather know what you both kept from me."

Who knew her first challenge would come so simply? "It was private, Dad, like my problems with Will." She dared not look at him. "I'm covered in dirt and need a shower. Do you want me to take Tony inside?"

"No." He disapproved of her desire for privacy. If only he knew the agony of the past three months. Thank God she'd never have to admit that, either.

She squeezed his arm, afraid to get close enough for him to hold her. She had to go inside before she out-and-out lied to her own dad.

"Iz-bell." Tony ran to her.

She hugged him against her legs but then pointed him toward her father. "Grandpa says you can slide with him."

Tony looked at his grandpa, who smiled. But George was so sad his smile seemed scary even to Isabel.

"Dad, really, it's nothing. Faith and I were friends as well as sisters. You know how it is with divorce. Sometimes friends choose sides."

"She wouldn't side against her own sister." His tone asked, *What did you do?*

He didn't ask out loud, and she couldn't explain, not without tarnishing her sister's reputation, or saying the one thing that would blow Tony and Ben's life to bits.

"It was trivial, Dad." She'd done it now, an outright falsehood. Tony whimpered, apparently catching her anxiety. "It's all right." She guided him toward her dad.

He tore away from her and ran back to the ladder and started to climb again. Frowning, her father went back to his station behind his grandson. "Why do you suppose he doesn't know your mother and me? I mean, we had a good time at the museums today, but when he got tired he started asking for the four of you."

"We were in and out of each other's houses all the time. Tony hasn't seen you as often as he saw me."

"It makes me feel funny," her father said. "I want him to love me as much as his mother did."

"He just has to get used to you." Which he would eventually do, if he lived with her mom and dad.

TRIVIAL. It almost made her cry as she scurried through the house, afraid of stumbling across another human. She'd actually managed to call Faith's infidelity with Will trivial. Where had she found the words? She longed to turn to her parents for comfort, but she couldn't without hurting their memories of her sister.

Upstairs, Isabel shucked off her clothes and climbed into the shower. She braced her hands against the tile and let water beat on her face and her head.

Here, she could cry without feeling weak, without troubling anyone else, without making anyone ask her what had gone wrong between her sister and her.

She'd never felt so alone, and she saw no relief in sight, with Ben ready to break all contact if she admitted what she knew about his son. And yet what could assuage her parents' sorrow for their older daughter more than the news that they alone had more right to him than their son-in-law?

She couldn't do it—couldn't betray Ben—couldn't ruin Tony's life. Not even for her parents.

After her shower the noises and scents of supper cooking drifted to her while she dressed. Her mom must have tried pot roast.

Isabel had worked hard. She was hungry enough to eat a good meal, but she'd never needed more time alone. She wasn't used to guarding every word she said.

A knock on her door startled her. "Come in," she said, bundling her dirty clothes into the basket Faith had so thoughtfully provided in her guest bath.

"What's up?"

Ben.

"This is getting to be a habit. Did you tell my parents you were coming up here?"

"Your mom sent me to bring you down before her pot roast dries out."

She laughed with relief at her mother acting normal. "Let me comb my hair. Has Dad brought Tony in?"

"They're sharing a hot chocolate." He shut the door. "Your father said to leave you alone. He seemed to think you were upset."

She eased a comb through her hair. "He asked me about Faith." The comb caught on a wet tangle, giving her an excuse to concentrate on it rather than Ben. "I had to lie."

"About?"

"Faith told him I was angry with her. Do you believe that? I was angry with her?"

"I believe. She and Will got used to covering their tracks. Nothing would have stopped them by the end."

"Yeah, I don't want to be like that."

"I'm afraid you couldn't be." He shook his head. Naturally, it would be easier for him if she was at home with lying. "I wonder if they really loved each other."

"The way they couldn't love you and me?"

"Yeah," he said. "Maybe when it's real, you'll do anything to be with the other person."

"They weren't even faithful to each other." She assumed Faith had still slept with Ben, though she'd chop off her own tongue before she'd ask. "Why not just beat ourselves with baseball bats? I've had it with Faith and Will. I don't want to talk about them." She slammed the comb on the bathroom counter and turned, shaking back her hair. "To tell you the truth, I'm just pissed because I still wonder what's wrong with me."

Ben looked her up and down. He'd better not be finding flaws, too. "Wrong with you?" he asked, his voice strangely hoarse.

"My own husband didn't want me." Her anger disintegrated, and she nearly cried again.

"Forget him." Ben took her in his arms. He pressed his lips to her hair, and instantly everything felt different.

Ben surrounded her with safety. His scent made her dizzy. She stared at his skin, smooth but masculine, his strong throat, pale from the winter sun, pulsing with life's blood. Pulsing too fast.

"Ben?" She tipped her head back to look into his face, but he tried to twist his head away. "Ben?"

Holding her hand against his cheek, she made him look at her. His mouth, strong and straight and so true, was not for her.

"Why should I forget about Will?"

"Isabel, stop." He tried to push her away, but she held on. She'd backed away from Will at the first sign of rejection. He'd trained her well for living with a man who loved elsewhere. But maybe some man could want her? The question whispered in her mind. Was she really so unlovable?

"Kiss me, Ben." She put her need into words. "We can't hurt anyone."

"We hurt each other every day. And there's Tony."

She watched his pulse jerk a few seconds more. He grabbed her wrists and tried to push her away. She didn't struggle, but he must have seen her distress.

"I won't play second string to Will anymore." He rubbed his knuckles on his cheek where she'd touched him. "Especially not for you."

"What did Faith have that I lack?" The words, out loud—how had she asked them out loud?—mortified her. She turned her back on Ben. Once again she'd thrown herself at a man who couldn't want her. "My God. I'm sorry. You loved her. She was your son's mother—and my sister. I'm sorry."

He turned her. She closed her eyes, too ashamed to look at him, but his arms went around her, roughly, as if he couldn't help himself. When she looked, he was leaning down.

With urgency she'd never known, Isabel met his mouth. She opened to him, baring her pain and loneliness. His husky groan made her legs tremble. She basked in the heat that fed on itself, a living fire.

He flattened his palms on each side of her head and twisted her face so that he could kiss her again and again and again until she was dizzy and moaning into his mouth, pliant, aching, willing to break any vow, destroy any promise for more of him.

This fire could destroy Ben and her and a friendship she'd cherished for more than a decade.

She grasped his wrists and stopped him. He stumbled back. Books talked about women who looked as if they'd been kissed. Ben looked kissed. Desire tightened his face, tempting her.

"I don't know when I started wanting to do that." His voice belonged to a stranger. She'd never heard sexual need in Ben's tone—because he'd belonged to her sister. "Isabel, do you want me to apologize?"

"No." She linked her fingers with his, terribly aware of the door at her back and her parents downstairs with his son. "You're not Will's second anything. I wanted *you*—not because of him."

His breathing remained harsh. "That's what I was trying to show you, that needing to touch you had nothing to do with Faith."

The enormity of what they'd just done shook them both. "You were still married to Faith before she died. It's too soon to know what you want."

"Our sex life had been sporadic for years. She probably felt she was being unfaithful to Will."

She knew all about living in that kind of wasteland. She hurt for him, but she had to protect herself, too. Neither of them was young enough or healthy enough to pretend this meant more than it did. She felt herself blushing. "We might both be desperate for a little satisfaction."

His smile stopped her, all male, laughing at her, but his need still disturbing. "So much for not letting Will stop you from trusting."

"I don't trust rebound attraction. I'm not asking you never to touch me again, but I have to know you're holding me, not getting back at Faith."

Pain flared across his face, but then he kissed her again, a blessing, mouth to mouth. A promise of pleasure and peace.

Strange. She'd never wanted peace in a man's arms.

"Isabel," he said as he lifted his head.

"We need distance and time to think." She staggered, but the direction she took, away from Ben, was wise.

From three feet away, his body exerted a hold on her. His shoulders, tense, his legs parted as if he were on guard. With his troubled, turbulent expression, he looked like a man who wanted a woman. He wanted her. "Do I sound confused?"

She shook her head, unhappy and yet alive. Blood-pumping, heart-thumping, restless-and-desperate-for-Ben's-touch alive. "I know your secrets and you know mine. I'm relieved I still feel desire for anyone, and knowing you need me, too, is a gift." She tried to smile. "But you have to be confused."

"You're used to living with Will." He turned and

left. But he didn't go downstairs. The door to his room closed softly.

Isabel wrapped her arms around her bedpost. He couldn't face her parents yet, either.

BEN WAITED outside the bathroom where his son was splashing, fit to flood the house. After dinner, Ben had gone outside to shovel the driveway and work Isabel out of his system. Coming upstairs after he'd finished, he'd recognized the sounds of Tony bathing, but he wasn't sure who was helping his son.

He took a deep breath and squared his shoulders, trying to feel normal again. How did a man force himself to feel normal?

He shoved the door open. Across alternating squares of black-and-white tile, Amelia looked up from the side of the wide, round tub. Tony scooped up bubbles in a foam dump truck and offered them.

Laughing came easy after all. "Isn't that water getting cold yet?" All big smiles and no worries, he knelt beside Amelia on the towel beside the tub.

"We've warmed it a couple of times," she said. "Is Isabel all right?"

"I don't know. I haven't seen her." He squeezed out his son's favorite airplane sponge to fly it around the boy's head. "Did you think something was wrong at dinner?"

"I thought you had something on your mind, too."

"I know how she feels. We've both lost a spouse."

"What happened between her and Will?"

Before he could answer, Tony squirted them both with the sponge. Ben poured a bucket of water over his son's shoulder and Tony crowed with joy.

"You won't tell me?"

"Even if I knew—" he suddenly shared Isabel's reluctance for lying to her mom "—it's none of my business. You should ask Isabel."

"We haven't talked about personal matters for a long time. You and Will and our girls were a self-contained unit, and none of you needed anyone else." She pushed soap bubbles off her arm, into the tub. "Leah thought so, too. She called me once to talk about it."

Leah and Amelia had talked? He nearly fell into the tub. "I didn't realize you were friends."

"We both missed our children. Don't get me wrong. I'm glad you had each other, but my daughters both changed after they married."

"Trust me," he said, wary as she came too close to the truth, "no one makes up for real family."

"I'm sorry, Ben. I'm so focused on my own troubles I forgot your parents had died."

Soon after he and Faith were married, when carbon monoxide had leaked into their town house. He never talked about it.

Nodding at Amelia, he flew the plane again and landed it on his son's shoulder. Tony dunked it, and then he started loading it with anything that would float on top of it.

"Where do you think Will and Faith were going?" Amelia asked.

She must be recovering from her grief. In shock, she'd asked no questions. Fortunately, Isabel had already prepared him for this conversation.

"Faith didn't call me or leave a note. I assumed she was heading out to visit you. She did that sometimes, and then she'd call me along the way."

"With Will?" He couldn't mistake her eagerness as she leaned forward.

"If he had a business trip in the area. Remember that time he drove her and Tony to Pittsburgh and she caught the train from there?"

"Oh, yeah. That's what I thought. It makes sense."

Only if you were really motivated to believe in Faith. For the first time, Ben took some of Amelia's sadness on himself. He might have to be cruel to protect his son, but Amelia had lost her older child already. He felt empathy. He hugged her, holding his wet hand away from her shoulder.

Tony pushed the plane and all its passengers under the water, finished for the night. With a yawn, he lifted both arms, and Ben pulled a towel off the warming rack. He scooped him out of the tub. "I'll finish here, Amelia. You should rest. This house and our meals aren't your responsibility."

"I like being useful." She kissed Tony's forehead.

"Maybe having all of us here comforts him when he's missing Faith."

Guilt covered Ben like the chilling water in his son's tub. "Soon he'll have to make do with only his old dad," Ben said. "I'm all he'll have."

Amelia's frown worked beneath his skin like a splinter. "He'll always have his grandpa and me and his aunt Isabel, too. We all have to keep his memories of his mom alive for him."

Ben couldn't seem to move. He pressed his cheek to Tony's head, and his son burrowed into his chest, full, clean and ready to sleep. Amelia eyed him oddly. He must look as if he'd swallowed that airplane sponge. At last, she tucked the towel closer around Tony and left. Ben began to breathe again.

She'd be more unhappy if she knew Faith had really been running away with Will, apparently on some crazy faux honeymoon. This time, it was kinder not to explain.

"Mommy?" Tony asked, as if he sensed sharpness in the air. "Iz-bell?"

"You're stuck with me, buddy." Ben produced his best grin and quickly dressed Tony in pajamas. "Want to read a story?"

"Tain." Tony owned just about every picture book ever written about trains. At bedtime he listened to any of them as if he'd never heard the story before.

Ben sat in a cushion-strewn rocker, cuddling his son and a SpongeBob pillow. Tony opened the book and pointed at the trains, chattering his own story. Ben tossed a couple of the cushions on the floor and then rested his chin on his son's head, agreeing whenever Tony stopped to wait for an answer.

Their nightly ritual comforted him as much as his son. At last, Tony turned back to the first page and nudged Ben. His turn. Reading, he almost forgot everything except the boy in his arms.

Almost. Amelia's wan face, and her curiosity about Faith's last day, stuck with him.

CHAPTER SEVEN

"I'M CHECKING out a couple of day-care centers this morning," Ben said the second Isabel reached the kitchen.

She twisted both hands in her mussed hair. All night long, that kiss had replayed in her head. Her pulse still hadn't slowed to normal. She felt hungover. She had to stop letting a man matter more to her than she did to him.

"Will you come with us?" he asked. "Two heads have to be better than one. We never used day care, and I don't trust myself to decide."

She wrapped both hands around the cup of coffee he handed her, feeling as cloudy as the dark gray sky in the window behind him. "I've never picked out a day care before. You should ask George and Amelia."

"You'll be able to tell if Tony's happy."

"So can you, and Faith and I agreed on one thing. We didn't like day care. I already hate the idea of him being left with strangers."

"Me, too." In fact, Ben's eyes had taken on the shadows of that first day again. "But I have to go back to work next Monday." He sipped from his own mug. "Unless I call in and take another week off."

He'd obviously thought about doing just that. "Can you?" she asked.

He nodded. "Maybe I will. Tony's still adjusting and so are we."

"I didn't mean to be tactless. The best fix would be for me to take care of him."

"I know you can't." He emptied the coffee carafe into her cup and then started to wash it. "Come with me. I even thought he should be around children his own age more, but I can't be objective about Tony right now."

Another long drink of coffee fortified her to get even more involved in Ben and Tony's life. "I'll go if you don't mind waiting until they pick up Leah's things from my house."

"We'll drive over there first." His mouth widened in a bona fide smile, and his relief touched her. He might not be concerned about a kiss whose memory left her feeling hollow, but he cared about her opinion. "Maybe if we find a place he likes, and I take him for short visits, he'll adjust."

"That's a good idea." She pulled a chair away from the table and sat, putting her mug on the glass top. "He's still asleep?"

"We read an extra book or two last night." Ben sounded self-conscious about his weakness for his son. Faith had always accused him of caring more about his job. Faith had been wrong. He loved his family best.

"Are you and I okay?" Isabel asked.

He glanced down the hall, as if her parents might come busting in the door.

"You regret it?" It hurt, but he was right to. They couldn't repeat last night's confusing kisses.

"I feel—odd." He knelt beside her chair, hemming her in. "But I still want…" He stopped, his frown signaling confusion like hers. "I'm not sorry." His hand dropped onto her knee, warm, heavy.

She stared at his long fingers. How many times had they touched each other? She was a naturally affectionate person. He always had been, too, but she'd never felt a single inappropriate vibe.

A terrible truth hit her. Kissing him, enjoying the unexpected, heady pleasure of his arms around her, hadn't felt inappropriate.

"An affair with you would be the perfect revenge," she said.

He sat back. "I'm revenge?"

"How can I know for sure? I keep thinking you just found out about Faith and Will. You're angry because of Tony. I might be the best way for you to pay them back."

"Do you know how many times I asked Faith to see a counselor?" His hand tightened on her knee. "She didn't want to make our marriage work. She wanted Will."

"But you wanted her."

"Because I'm a decent man. I married Faith. We had Tony, and I never doubted he was mine. I wanted my family to survive."

"She still matters to you, and she should." Isabel touched his shoulder, smoothing his shirt, loving the warmth of him beneath the coarse material. "I don't want to ruin my friendship with you, trying to get back at our cheating spouses."

"Do you still care about Will?"

"I think I'm over him, but then something happens—I uncover some new secret, and I'm hurt all over again."

"But are you still in love with him?"

"You're grilling me." She didn't blame him. "I don't know all the answers." She grabbed her cup. Coffee spilled over the lip, onto her index finger. Ben quickly took the mug.

"Does it burn?" He set the cup down as he brought her hand to his mouth. He sucked the hot coffee off, and Isabel shuddered at the sight and the feel of his lips against her skin. His mouth lingered. He looked into her eyes, and she sank against him.

"Stop." Yet she slid her hands around his neck, her body hardly her own.

"Holding you doesn't feel wrong."

She felt his lips in her hair, at her temple. His heart thudded against her face as she tried to move away.

Frustration made her clumsy. "It would if Mom and Dad came in."

"Because we don't want to hurt them, and they couldn't understand."

"*I* don't understand." Ben was the last man she'd expected to… "And that sounds like an excuse Will and Faith would have latched onto."

He lifted his head, searching his own motives. "Maybe."

A thud from Tony's room dictated their next move.

"He's emptying his crib. I have to go up." Ben looked back at her as he went to the door. "Don't assume what we feel is wrong, Isabel."

Without his arms around her, his hungry mouth seeking hers, she felt cold, more alone than ever. Thunder rattled the house, so in tune with her mood it felt like punctuation. "How can I believe we're right?"

KEEPING AN EYE on Tony while interviewing the caregivers at one day care after another left Ben no time to dwell on his baffling feelings for Isabel. The first center was too crowded. The moment they stepped inside the next one, Isabel wrinkled her nose and turned him around.

"They obviously don't change diapers often enough." She pushed him through the glass door, making Tony laugh at her over his dad's shoulder. "I can't stand to think of him with a dirty diaper."

"He's almost potty trained."

"Hygiene is a big deal, Ben."

"One of the biggest." He smiled. Her grin reminded him of old times as she hung on to Tony's hand.

"Where to next?" she asked.

"The Children's Cottage." He pulled the pages he'd printed from his Internet search out of his pocket and looked for the address. "On Bradley and Melton."

"I haven't heard of that one."

"You mean with all the children you've had to place in day care?"

"Don't make fun." She peered at the information page. "I mean shouldn't we stick to national chains?"

"We need to find a place that feels safe and offers a good student-to-teacher ratio." He kissed his son's cold-flushed cheek. "And don't forget the smell-good factor."

"Ha-ha." Isabel took the keys he'd looped around his finger and opened the back door of his car. "In you go, Tony."

He went, grabbing a water bottle as he scrambled into his seat. Isabel popped the bottle's top open for him while Ben buckled him in.

"We make a good team." He felt underhanded as he stealthily breathed in her scent.

She wrapped Tony's hands around the water bottle and moved away. "Daddy may have lost his mind."

"Daddy." Tony beamed around his drink. He took a quick sip and then offered it to Ben.

Ben drank and then wiped his mouth with the back of his hand. "True love means you don't worry about pretzel crumbs."

"Thanks for the warning." She took her place in the front. "Ready for this cottage place?"

He patted Tony's happily kicking foot and then took his own seat behind the steering wheel. "You're in a good mood."

"I like a task. We have places to be, important matters to consider."

"Other than ourselves?"

"Exactly."

She folded her hands in her lap, and he tried not to laugh at her prim posture. She'd been anything but prim in his arms. He couldn't help wondering if last night had been an anomaly. Couldn't resist wanting to kiss her again.

But Tony came first.

The Children's Cottage looked good. Maybe too good from the outside. Brick building and chintz curtains. Clean playground equipment in the side yard. Children's laughter floated through the windows.

His heart beat faster from excitement and fear. This might be the place where he left his son. He liked the sounds of happiness, but those strangers Isabel had mentioned earlier spooked him.

"It's almost too good to be true after the other places," Isabel said.

Shouldn't there be a test to determine whether a day care was safe? "It'd be more helpful if you'd convince me he won't feel abandoned."

"Sorry. I can't help being afraid something will happen to him. Maybe because of the accident." She took Tony from him as he opened the front door.

"Could you back off?" She looked surprised, and Ben regretted the harsh question. "I'm already worried, and I wonder if you're looking for reasons to turn these places down."

"Maybe." She bumped affectionately into his arm. "I told you I feel funny about handing him over." She squeezed her nephew so hard he grunted, but then laughed.

Ben's heart melted.

Faith would have snapped back at him. Isabel understood give-and-take. Comparing Isabel with Faith would never have occurred to him in a millennium before. He focused on the job at hand.

Inside, they met Mrs. Nash, the center director, who was thrilled to give them a tour. The reception area, behind shatterproof glass, sat in the middle of the building. The rooms around it were more like oversize cubicles, except for the "baby room" the center's director showed them to.

"We have full walls in here to afford the children more quiet. Tony would spend nap time here. Otherwise, the toddlers use that cubicle." Mrs. Nash pointed at an open area in the west corner. "Let's show Tony his classroom."

Halfway there, Isabel's phone rang. She pulled it out of her pocket and read the number. "It's Ray." Whatever she and her attorney were cooking up obviously made her uncomfortable. "I should answer it," she said.

Nodding, Ben took Tony, who held out both arms for "My Iz-bell, my Iz-bell!"

She came back to hug him and Ben fought his own compulsion to keep Isabel at his side. "I'll be at the front door, sweetie. You can see me through the windows."

"Doesn't like to leave his mommy?" Mrs. Nash asked.

"I'm his aunt." Isabel looked at Ben, her face serious. As clearly as if she'd said the words out loud, he heard her thought. *If only I were Tony's mom.*

Or maybe the wish came from his own fear.

"RAY, HEY. Thanks for calling back so quickly." She tried to sound all-business, but her head was back in that rainbow-strewn hall with Ben and her nephew. If only she were Tony's mom. If only she and Ben were his family. It was what they both craved. Unlike Will and Faith, they'd risk anything to keep from tearing their family apart.

The Harlequin Reader Service® — Here's how it works:

NO POSTAGE
NECESSARY
IF MAILED
IN THE
UNITED STATES

BUSINESS REPLY MAIL
FIRST-CLASS MAIL   PERMIT NO. 717-003   BUFFALO, NY

POSTAGE WILL BE PAID BY ADDRESSEE

HARLEQUIN READER SERVICE
3010 WALDEN AVE
PO BOX 1867
BUFFALO NY 14240-9952

But Ben could hardly know what he wanted right now, and she was no better for Tony than her parents. He needed to be with the only father he'd known.

She needed to know if she could make a life on her own. The chance to settle scores with Faith and Will must be at the root of her attraction to Ben. That was no foundation on which to build a baby boy's home.

"I've made plans for Tony's trust fund, and I need to talk over the rest of Will's papers with you," Ray said.

"I've read the copies he left at home."

"Your wishes change some of his provisions. I have to be certain you understand what you're giving away."

"Nothing that belongs to me."

Ray was silent, but she sensed his disapproval. "When can you come by the office? Tomorrow morning?"

"Sure. What time?"

"We'll have breakfast. You show up and I'll provide all."

"And Ben?"

"Maybe just you this time."

Good. She didn't mind putting off another disagreement with Ben. She'd have to fight him to make him accept Tony's legacy.

"Bring a pen. I have a stack of papers for you to initial before we do the finals." He paused as if reluctant to go on. "You won't believe who called me."

"Who?"

"Leah Barker." He chuckled. "She wanted to know if her attorney should look over any documents her son left in my care."

"That woman." Her new leaf, being kind to Leah, had browned rather quickly.

"Will had to inherit his control issues from someone."

"Thanks for not being upset."

"With you? Leah's always been inappropriate where Will was concerned. You're trying to do the right thing. I'm more concerned you'll cheat yourself with good intentions."

"Not while you're in my corner. See you in the morning."

"Try for eight o'clock. Give me a call if the traffic holds you up."

She went back inside, fuming over Leah, until the squishy carpet caught her attention. She tested it with a bounce. And another. A little guy could fall on this carpet and not break anything. She drifted past the other rooms, peering in at each door.

The caregivers, men and women of various ages, were all focused on the children. Playing games. Listening to stories. They paid attention as if they meant it, not as if this was a nine-to-five they had to endure.

She stopped at the toddlers' room. Ben and Mrs. Nash were talking while Tony pounded a toy drum at his dad's feet. Tony looked up.

"Iz-bell." He waved a rubber drumstick at her, and she sat beside him. Ben's swift, private smile let her believe she belonged with him and Tony.

Tony offered her one of his sticks and she tried to help him beat out a rhythm, until he grew exasperated with her lack of talent and snatched the stick back.

"Mrs. Nash, Isabel and I will talk about all this tonight, and I'll call you tomorrow." Ben included her in the decision. She liked mattering to him. "Thanks for everything."

Isabel stood, lifting Tony while Mrs. Nash gently harvested the drum set from his hands.

"You can play with this if you come back to visit us," she said. "I'll look forward to speaking with you again, too, Isabel."

Isabel nodded. She and Ben trooped outside. At the car, she helped Ben buckle Tony back into his seat. The baby offered her his water, and she faked a drink. Ben did his fatherly duty and took a real swallow, receiving a congratulatory grunt from his son.

They were quiet for the first few minutes of the drive home. Not home. The drive back to Faith's house.

"No more too-good-to-be-true jokes?" Ben asked.

"I'm sorry about that." She turned so only he could hear. "I panicked."

"I know." He turned onto the interstate. "But if Tony were your child?"

"Don't worry. I'm not planning on losing my mind and snatching him away from you." Her heart tapped out a frightened beat. It was too easy and too good to picture herself as Tony's mother.

Ben nodded, relief unmistakable, despite his apparent effort to neither smile nor frown. "What about when you have your own children?"

"After seven years under Will's thumb, I'm making my own life. I couldn't be a dependent mom so I'll have to work outside the house."

"What would you have done if you'd had a child with Will? No." He wiped his mouth. "I'm sorry. I won't ask that."

Because his wife had been the mother of Will's child. Isabel chewed on her thumbnail, trying to look as if the reminder didn't cut her deep.

Ben wasn't malicious. He'd gone out of his way to help her with the house. He'd exposed his uncertainty about the day-care center. She owed him a what-if. Besides, she'd planned the maternal phase of her life with intricate detail. She already knew what crib she'd want in the nursery, the pattern she'd choose for drapes, the brand of diaper her baby would wear.

"If I'd had a child with Will, and he'd never loved Faith, I would have counted myself the luckiest stay-at-home mom in the world."

"I figured. Why was Faith so restless? She didn't want Tony in day care, but she wasn't satisfied being a stay-at-home mom."

"Faith wasn't satisfied—period. We were different—neither of us wrong, just different. And I've changed, too."

"Because of Will. Maybe we shouldn't talk about it. Not in front of him, anyway." He nodded toward the rearview mirror.

"You're right." She had no interest in Ben's current feelings for her sister. "Who knows how much he takes in? That cottage seemed like a nice place."

"I think so, too. Tony had a good time."

"What happens next?" she asked.

"I suggested he and I visit again, while you were talking with Ray, and Mrs. Nash agreed."

"Cool." She still had doubts. "We're both novices, Ben. Maybe you should ask someone with a child what she does for day care."

"We love Tony. That makes us experts. Working parents do this all the time."

"It's terrifying. I'd be happier with a police report on everyone who works there. You should ask Mom to visit."

He flashed a relieved smile. "That's a good idea. She already seems stronger, but I'd like her to feel involved with Tony."

He surprised her. "Why?"

"She's trying her best to be a good grandma, but I think you and I assumed she saw more of Tony than she did. Faith and Will must have risked using your mother as an excuse to leave town together."

"You're sure of that now?" The possibility had hurt enough.

"I know Tony. He likes hanging out with your mom and dad, but he prefers having you or me around, too. If he'd spent as much time as Faith claimed with your parents, he'd know them better."

This morning's comfortable solidarity departed.

Isabel scooted back in her seat.

All the more reason to be smarter than Faith and resist her attraction to Ben. He'd said last night had changed them. It didn't have to. Was she about to lose her head over a few passionate kisses? She'd never forget nor regret them, but it was like Ben always said. Tony came first.

If she lost Ben, she might lose Tony, too.

"WHAT DO YOU THINK, Amelia?" Ben asked.

She looked up from the brochure she'd read front to back. "I'd like to see the place in person."

He and Amelia were sharing the living room couch and coffee in china cups that felt too delicate for his big hands. "I'd appreciate your opinion. Do you want to drive over tomorrow? You can watch Tony with the other children and then check out the place with me on another tour."

"Sounds great." Smiling, she turned back to the front of the brochure. "Faith would be glad you asked me."

George, standing by the fireplace, sounded as if

he'd sucked coffee into his lungs. He bent toward the fire Ben had laid to take the chill off, but then he turned, his eyes unexpectedly warm for his wife. "You said her name the way you used to—not as if you wanted to die."

Ben exhaled and set his cup down. "We all have to talk about Faith normally," he said. "Or Tony won't remember her without the feelings we have for her now. He'll be better off if she's just his mom, not a saint."

"I know." Amelia took a sugar cube and dropped it into her coffee. "I keep praying someone made a mistake. That Will and she will suddenly stroll into the house—they'll want to know what we're doing here. Why Isabel is selling his things. Why we're running Faith's home."

Ben gritted his teeth to keep his mouth shut. He'd be tempted to kill Will if Amelia's fantasy came true.

George put both hands on Amelia's shoulders. "You're torturing yourself with ideas like that. And don't forget Isabel. She's been patient, but you don't want her to think Faith mattered more to you. We still have a daughter."

"And you have Tony." Even as he made himself say it—and mean it—Ben wished he could take his boy away.

Amelia leaned back, tears squeezing between her closed eyelids, as she rested against George's hands. Ben felt a father's empathy. Amelia needed her grandson, to remember a part of Faith would always be alive in Tony. He should have seen that before now.

"Where is our boy?" George's bluff tone rang false. "Isabel's putting him to bed tonight?"

"Naturally, Tony knows Isabel better than us, honey," Amelia said. "You're grieving for Faith, so you want to come first with him, but he loves us all, and we won't let so much time pass between visits from now on."

"You're welcome as long as you can stay," Ben said.

"Thanks." George returned to contemplating the mantel, and Ben suspected the other man resented being welcomed to his own daughter's home.

Ben had always assumed Amelia was more likely to want Tony, but he'd better keep an eye on George, too.

AFTER BREAKFAST with Ray the next morning, Isabel initialed so many papers her hand began to cramp.

"Leah's going to ask you about giving so much to Tony."

Isabel shuddered, a natural response to the chill that ran down her spine. "What does Leah have to do with my business?"

"She's posed one unseemly question after another. I've been less competently examined in court."

"You can tell her the truth about our plans before

she badgers us to death. Will claimed Tony as his nephew. Even she knows how seriously he took that responsibility."

"Which, I must confess, puzzled me until you explained their true relationship."

Isabel paused, pen in air. "Why? He was a responsible man. He ran a successful business. His employees counted on him. Why shouldn't a child?"

"Business came first with Will. Children? No. I never understood his interest in Tony. I thought he'd get bored."

"Not with his own son." Saying the words plied her barely closed wounds with a knife.

"Sorry, Isabel." Ray slid the next page under her pen. "And we need to talk about the business. I'm not sure why the officers over there haven't asked to meet with us. I've tried to give you breathing room, but we have to protect your interests."

"I don't have the experience to run Barker Synthetics. Tony's and my interests may take a dive unless I sell before my stewardship ruins the company."

Ray twisted his mouth. "I'll help you find someone capable."

"Even with help, I don't have the experience. The employees deserve better management."

"I wish you'd rethink." He stacked the papers still in front of him. "I'll arrange a meeting at the company. Make no decisions until we talk to your employees."

She stared at him. Not even a clock ticked in the silence of his office. "This isn't my world, Ray. I don't have to think it over." At last—an easy decision.

CHAPTER EIGHT

THE RAIN-WET STREETS had begun to freeze as Isabel drove the slippery black ribbon of road back to Ben's house that evening. Half-frozen, covered in more dust and dying for a cup of coffee, she parked in front of the garage and hurried up the front steps.

Tony's laughter echoed down the gold-wood stairs again. Dinner smells raised a ruckus in her empty belly. Dishes rattled from the kitchen, but she looked up, drawn to her nephew.

"Isabel?" her mother called from the kitchen. "Is that you?"

"Coming, Mom." She shouldn't make herself part of Tony's nighttime habits anyway. Amelia turned from the sink, a saucer dripping suds from her hands. "We tried to call you."

"I left my cell phone in the car." People were still calling to sympathize with her loss of Will. Hearing from her well-meaning friends was nice, but she felt like a phony, so she'd begun to ignore the house phone, too. "Did you have a good day with Tony?"

A smile lit her mom's eyes. Even her skin had more color tonight. "It was *fine*." She used the word the way they did in old movies. "Ben signed him up for the center you saw yesterday."

"I assumed there'd be a waiting list."

Her mother nodded, unconcerned. "Two siblings are probably moving, but Ben agreed to let George and me look after Tony until the list comes open."

"That could be months. You're willing to stay?"

"We don't mind. That other family is supposed to hear about the husband's transfer in the next few weeks."

A tinge of sadness colored Isabel's relief. "I guess he's really going to stay with someone else while Ben works."

Amelia seemed surprised. "Surely you didn't offer to look after Tony?"

Isabel shook her head. "You'd disapprove?"

"You've been our daughter and then Will's wife. You should be your own person for a while now, not Tony's caregiver."

Isabel agreed with her mother's reasons, but she added her deepening feelings for Ben to the caution. "Tony will be all right at The Children's Cottage, won't he?"

Amelia dried her hands and put one arm around her. "Your sister was lucky that you love her son as if he were yours."

These unintentional jabs were starting to get on

her nerves. "We were a family." One that Faith hadn't valued.

"I used to envy your closeness to Faith. A mother likes to think her daughter will come to her first with all her secrets." Amelia hugged her again, as if to soften a hint of accusation. "I wanted even her stories about everyday life, how she persuaded Tony to eat beets or keep his sneakers on when he hates to wear shoes."

"I thought you and she were closer, that she told you everything." Isabel held her breath. She'd offered the perfect opening if Faith had confided about Will.

With a hurt look and quick steps, her mother returned to the sink. "Apparently Faith didn't talk as much as either of us assumed." She began to wash a plate. "It's funny. When your child dies, you realize how little you knew about her. She left my house fourteen years ago for college, and she never lived under my roof again. She always told me exactly what she wanted me to know, nothing more. I can't figure out what she was doing in that car with Will. With their suitcases and Tony."

"I wish you'd stop worrying about it." She prayed her mother would let that loose thread go before she worried the truth out of it.

"She didn't call to say she was coming."

Answers would not bring her comfort. "She probably wanted to surprise you."

"She's done that before." Her mom sounded hopeful. Her hands stilled. "I guess we'll never know."

"It doesn't matter." Isabel linked her arms around her mom's neck. "She loved you. That's all you need to remember."

"It's not enough. I thought she was here, safe in her own home, and then the police called, and then Ben. My world collapsed." She realized what she'd said. "Not my whole world. I love you, Isabel. You know that?"

She nodded, swallowing tears.

"I'm not ignoring the fact that you've lost your sister, but I can't seem to understand what happened with Faith."

"What's to understand?" Instinctively, she looked for Ben, her guilt at keeping secrets so strong that she immediately worried her mother knew about Tony.

Thank goodness common sense took over. If her mom knew, she'd have said something.

Amelia went on, washing a large plate. "Faith changed over the years. She thought I was prying if I asked where she planned to go on vacation, what she'd done when she came back. She didn't want me to know what she spent for something as simple as a necklace I'd never seen before." Amelia handed Isabel the plate and Isabel began to dry. "I didn't care about the cost. I only asked if Ben gave it to her. I was glad she'd found a man who still remembered to surprise her after so many years of marriage."

Isabel concentrated on the plate, but she couldn't

hide from an image of Will, standing behind Faith fastening a necklace. Will had killed her love for him, but each possible new demonstration of his feelings for Faith hurt her. Why the hell had he gone after her sister?

"Ben often gave Faith jewelry." Small pieces, expensive ones, shiny bangles, as he'd once described them, that he thought Faith might like. However, Isabel wouldn't be asking Ben if he'd given Faith this necklace her mother was talking about.

"Why did questions make her so angry?" Amelia asked.

"I don't know." She couldn't lie anymore, and she wouldn't betray her sister to her mom.

"I wish I did. I can't forget strange moments like that. Maybe I should have pushed her."

"You have to forget, Mom. Haven't you seen how sad Dad is? Part of it comes from worrying about you." Isabel reached for the next plate. "You know there's a dishwasher?"

"I don't like to use them. Never have."

"You're a firm believer in taking the hard way."

"No machine washes a dish as well as I." She leaned on one foot to kiss her younger daughter's cheek. "Besides, I like having you beside me, helping."

Isabel held back another rush of tears. They'd all lost Faith. They all had to mourn and survive, but her mother would never learn the truth about Faith from her.

BEN SCRATCHED out his fourth false start at designing a tree house for his son. He scrunched up the paper and tossed it into the wastebasket beside his desk.

"What's that?"

He tensed at the sound of Isabel's voice, glad she'd come home but uneasy that he thought of her return as coming home. "Tony and I stopped at the builder's supply store for caulk today, and he saw some tree houses. I'd like to build one for him, but I seem to be better at chemistry than design."

"You can't build out there now. The ground's frozen." She came to his desk.

"The trees aren't," he said.

"He's only eighteen months old. It's early for tree climbing."

He laughed. She was right, but he wasn't a reckless father. "Calm down. I won't let him climb a tree, Isabel. He's not tall enough to reach a branch."

"Not tall enough to—what's wrong with you?" She slumped into the fat leather chair beside him.

"After a day with Amelia, I feel all but inept. She changes diapers one-handed, offers Tony a drink before he even knows he's thirsty, and she quizzed Mrs. Nash as if the poor woman was up for senate confirmation."

With an affectionate laugh, Isabel kicked off her shoes and pulled her feet into the chair.

"By the time we left The Children's Cottage, I expected them to offer her a job."

"But that should be good. Don't you feel better about signing him up now?"

"What if I proved she'd be a better choice to raise Tony than I am?" He sat back, almost sick at putting his worst fears into words.

Isabel tightened her arms around her legs, a picture of defensiveness. "We could tell the truth and explain. Then you wouldn't have to be so concerned."

He stared, shocked, dismayed. "Every time you bring this up, you scare me."

"My mother just asked me some questions about Faith that I couldn't answer. She and Dad might make the right choice, but either way, I don't like trying to put my mom off the scent."

"You make it sound as if taking this small chance would make us all one big happy family." He shook his head. "What's to stop them from deciding they want Faith's child, and they have more right to raise him than a man who's no blood relation at all?"

"What have Mom and Dad ever done to make you think they're capable of that? You are Tony's father."

"In your eyes. In Faith's, I was the guy she was leaving." He dragged his pencil in a short deep line that tore through the top sheet of paper. "Your parents could easily persuade themselves they feel the same."

"So you're building tree houses?"

Isabel, his accomplice, seemed on the verge of breaking. "You're tired." Wan with exhaustion was more like it. "Let's argue when we're not likely to lose our tempers."

"I'm too restless to sleep."

He took a second look at her. She was restless and she'd come to sit with him? "What are your mom and George doing?"

"I don't know. Reading the paper in the living room. Are you trying to get rid of me?"

"No." His strange new emotions for Isabel troubled him almost as much as the chance that she might let something slip about Tony.

He'd like to lean across the corner of his desk and ease the tension from her vulnerable mouth. Her skin, so soft, seemed to have bewitched him. Ever since he'd kissed her, he'd dreamed of touching her again.

They couldn't talk about that. Not without trust neither of them felt. She wanted him to tell the truth, and his worst fear was that she would. If he was smart, he'd start looking for reasons to send George and Amelia back to Pennsylvania and Isabel back to her own house.

He couldn't do it. Tony liked having his Iz-bell with him, and the Deavers were getting to know Tony better.

He turned to the next blank page on his pad and

changed the subject. "Maybe I should try a house on a platform?"

"You can buy them."

"I want to give Tony something I've made with my own hands."

"You don't have to cover every father-and-son activity right now." She stood. "Ben, I know you better than you know yourself. You wouldn't be panicking over that graph paper—" she pointed "—if you weren't afraid you're doing the wrong thing, too."

As she walked out, her scent, suddenly so familiar and seductive, wafted his way. His feet moved as he tried to follow, without a rational thought in his head.

"Night, Ben." She didn't look back.

He stared after her, dull-witted. He half stood but sank back down. He was forcing Isabel to lie. And he needed her to choose him and Tony over her own parents. How could any woman resist?

THE NEXT DAY, Isabel opened Will's sock drawer and burst into tears. She cried over the thought of folding his socks and putting them away. She'd believed she'd been his wife, his true love, had liked the intimacy of doing small things for him. Putting socks away didn't seem so intimate when she considered he'd probably hired someone to do it after she'd left.

The doorbell pealed and she jumped, but then she

slammed the drawer shut and flew down the stairs, hoping she'd find Ben. Her fierce need to see him worried her, as if beyond her control, she cared more than she should. She wiped her eyes and yanked the front door open.

No Ben. It was Leah.

She looked far from prostrate. Leah was wearing her I'll-fight-to-the-last-breath-for-my-son expression. A familiar sight during Isabel's marriage.

"Leah."

The other woman gathered the lapels of a black wool coat that looked as chic on her as it would have on the thirty-year-younger women for whom it had been designed. "You aren't glad to see me."

"I'm surprised. You didn't feel well."

"I thought you might need help—" she stepped inside, urging Isabel backward "—with my son's things."

"Didn't the delivery service bring your china—and other stuff?"

Leah nodded, but she searched the hall and wandered toward the first doorway, peering inside. She wanted more. "I noticed few of Will's belongings in the shipment."

Isabel shook her head at her former mother-in-law's back. In a normal relationship, she might have expected "I gave you that china. It's yours still." With Leah, she was lucky she hadn't had to sign a receipt.

Isabel shut the door with zest. "Back in battle mode?"

"You and Will intended to end your marriage. Surely I'm more entitled to my son's things than you."

Normally as warm and fuzzy as a porcupine, Will's death seemed to have sent Leah over an unhealthy edge. Isabel smiled—with a touch of rage. "He didn't mention giving you everything he owned in his will, but I'm in the middle of sorting his socks. Maybe you'd like to finish?"

Leah whirled, and the coat spread with a dramatic flourish she would have loved to see in a mirror. Her concern had nothing to do with Isabel's sarcasm. "What are you doing with his clothing?"

"Packing them for Goodwill. What would you do with his clothes?"

"He was my son, Isabel." Her pain was real—and savage. The suffering of any mother who'd lost her son. Leah would never be Isabel's best friend, but she couldn't turn her back on the other woman's pain. Especially since it seemed to be having an unhinging effect.

"You should have come to the funeral, Leah. You needed to say goodbye." She'd never run Will's life again. He'd evaded her clutches once and for all.

"I'm here now. Why don't I finish his room for you?"

"No." Her short surge of sympathy faded. No Barker would ever steamroll her again. "We can work together if you like. I still have things in our room, as well."

"What are you doing with your belongings?"

"Culling whatever I won't need in a smaller place." She started up the stairs ahead of Leah, biting her tongue instead of reminding Will's mom her own belongings were off-limits. "Feel free to hang your coat in the closet."

"I'll keep it. This place feels like ice. You can't afford to heat?"

Isabel looked up at the tall ceilings, down at the cold, marble-topped table and the roses that hadn't been changed since she'd released the cleaning woman three days ago. Then she stared at her own pinkish hands. "I didn't notice."

Leah paused at the upstairs thermostat to turn up the heat. Isabel hurried, using the moment to keep back one of Will's watches and a platinum signet ring he'd worn often. She wanted them for Tony since they'd meant something to his birth father.

Leah stopped in the bedroom doorway. "What are you taking?"

Like a thief caught in the act, Isabel turned from the small cedar box where Will had kept his jewelry. "I'm giving Tony a couple of pieces."

"Tony? He was only Will's nephew."

Isabel saw red. She'd had no idea that could actually happen, but a scarlet haze formed around Leah. She didn't understand the woman's determination to own everything her son had touched.

"Where do you plan to stay, Leah?"

"Not here?"

"I'm still at Ben's."

"I don't mind sleeping in my child's house alone."

Isabel had always backed down when Leah took this kind of stance because Will hated scenes, but even Leah had never been so audacious.

"You'll be more comfortable in a hotel." Isabel made sure Leah knew she was serious. "I'll make a reservation for you."

"No—"

"No problem at all." Isabel interpreted Leah's beginning to her own advantage. She slipped the watch and ring she'd chosen into her pocket and went to the phone. Getting the number for a nearby hotel was easy. She made a reservation for Leah. Isabel left it open-ended, though she'd love to send the woman packing this very minute.

By the time she turned, Leah had already closed the lid on the cedar box and slid it to one end of the long dresser, staking her claim.

"Leah, you and I are going to argue if you don't control your possessiveness."

"You were divorcing my son."

"He sent no papers, and I never filed. I've already returned every object you put in our hands."

"I want my son's things, too. I have nothing to remember him by."

Her strident voice cracked. Isabel wanted to be anywhere but in this house. "I'm trying to understand, but you're being selfish." And extreme enough to make Isabel wary.

Tears wet Leah's cheeks. She covered her face with her hands. The precious gems her husband had given her throughout their marriage glittered on her fingers. She'd always worn her net worth. "I loved him, Isabel. You obviously didn't at the end. Why should you keep the things he loved?"

Isabel felt like a fool—again. She'd tried to soften toward Leah after the other woman's talk of staying close. The Barkers always managed to dupe her. "I don't want anything. I've only kept a few of Will's things for Tony. And you know he loved our nephew with all his heart."

Leah nodded, but her head moved as if it weighed about four tons. "I should have first claim. By the time he died, I was his closest relation."

Bitter words tickled the tip of Isabel's tongue. Will would have burned everything he'd owned before he'd have left it to Leah. He'd always felt she'd surrounded him like an affectionate python.

Isabel hung to her temper, barely. "Choose anything you want from these boxes and bags. Goodwill picks up the rest tomorrow."

Leah's own anger flashed, so near hatred Isabel stepped back. "Thanks."

"I'll go downstairs." A shower to flush off the venom would be impractical. "Take what you want."

Here was her mom at home, doing anything to get

to know Tony better, cooking and cleaning no matter how many times Ben tried to persuade her to relax. Of course, she already knew Tony was her grandson. But Leah's behavior—smash and grab—made a better case for Ben than anything he'd ever suggested.

She was crossing the hall when the doorbell rang again. She opened up to cool air and a tall man in a perfect suit. Lovely bronze-and-red-striped tie. Tanning-bed complexion.

"Ms. Jordan?"

Faith's name. Isabel grabbed the doorjamb. Pain, hah. She'd suffered nothing before this moment. This smarmy-looking man expected Faith to be at home in her house.

He went on. "I'm Neal Lofton. Mr. Barker told me to expect you'd be here. I've come to value the house." He slipped her a business card as if he were passing her the keys to the kingdom.

She stared at the card, but she couldn't even read his name. All she could focus on was Leah, upstairs, longing to own all of Will's prized possessions. She'd love to take over the sale of this house.

"Barker." She barely managed to say her own name. Apparently, her answer confused Mr. Lofton. He stared as if she'd sprouted a few spare heads. She felt as if hers had swollen, along with her tongue. "I'm Isabel Barker. I can't talk right now. I have a visitor upstairs, and my husband passed away last week. Can we meet some other time, please?"

"Passed—Mr. Barker died?"

She nodded while the possibilities clicked through Lofton's gaze like drawings of fruit on a slot machine. "You still own the house, Mrs. Barker? Not Ms. Jordan?"

"My name is Isabel. Call me, and we'll meet again. I can't talk now." Her manners stretched to breaking point. Beyond. She grabbed the door and swung it. Lofton disappeared behind the highly polished wood.

"You can't sell my son's house."

Great. How foolish had she been, thinking she'd get away without Leah overhearing? She'd no doubt rushed to the stairs to eavesdrop.

"Leah, this is my house. Face it. Will would have had to ask my permission to sell." She turned, so angry she felt at no disadvantage having to look up at Leah. "We didn't divorce. We didn't discuss divorce. I left after my husband told me he loved another woman. That's where our marriage stood. If you can't let this fight go I'll have to ask you to leave."

Leah considered, visibly weighing her options.

Isabel clutched the last ounce of civility she might ever muster. She'd never lost a child, but Will had spent his adult life putting up barricades, dodging his mother's searching grasp. This was Leah's last sick

struggle to touch the things that had been touched by
her son.

Isabel didn't understand her, but she'd spent three
months wondering why Will hadn't wanted her, too.

She headed for the kitchen. There had to be a
drink stronger than coffee in those cupboards.

Instead of searching, Isabel turned to another possible addiction. She picked up the phone and started
to dial Ben. He'd understand how the real-estate
agent had cut her legs out from under her, and that
Leah seemed to have lost her mind. A woman shared
these blows with her best friend.

She set down the phone. A woman only shared if her
life hadn't turned into a bad remake of *Peyton Place*.

BEN STUMBLED out of the superstore with a cart full
of day-care necessities and Tony, clutching his new
SpongeBob sleeping mat. A sleeping mat. Ben had
never heard of such a thing, but when a saleslady had
shown him and Tony a section filled with them he'd
felt incompetent. Most dads should have been able
to figure out that one.

He and Tony had spent the day buying everything
on the list the day care had given them. And they'd
tacked on an hour in the pediatrician's office, for a
form that certified Tony'd had all his inoculations.

At the car, Ben opened the back. Tony let go of
his mat to grab his matching lunch box and back-
pack. All SpongeBob all the time.

"My Iz-bell." Tony snatched up the sleeping mat again and slapped it into Ben's face.

"Isabel's busy. We can't show her right now." Ben peeled the plastic wrap off the mat. If Tony kept hugging it so close, he was liable to smother himself.

"Bob," Tony said. "Iz-bell." He shook the mat. "Iz-bell."

Why not? Ben stared at his son, who suddenly seemed older and yet more vulnerable. How was he supposed to turn his small boy over to strangers? This would be a good time to let Isabel reassure him that he wasn't abandoning Tony.

He shoved the rest of their purchases into the back of his car and carried Tony to his car seat. Fastening it, he shifted the mat out of range and planted a kiss on his boy's head.

"We'll drive by. If she's busy, we go home."

Tony, all smiles, nodded, but Ben doubted he'd agree to leave without showing all his loot, even if Isabel was entertaining Barker Synthetics's board.

In front of her house, Ben spotted Leah's long, low, luxury car. Slightly mud-spattered but still reeking of good living. "I'm glad you thought of coming, Tony."

"Iz-bell!"

"She'll need us."

Ben parked and turned to the backseat to let his son out. Clutching his mat, Tony stood on the seat and held out both arms for everything else. He clenched and unclenched his reaching fists. "Bob."

Searching the windows for screaming women or shattered glass, Ben didn't respond fast enough.

"Bob, Daddy."

"Okay, Son." He took the mat and carried Tony to the back of the SUV. He slipped the mat back into the bag and carried boy and SpongeBob plunder to the house, intent on being a buffer between Leah and Isabel.

He drummed on the door, but then turned the handle and walked straight in.

"Iz-bell." Tony's voice rattled the rafters.

Ben laughed at his son's lung power.

Isabel came out of the kitchen at a run. Ben registered the shock that froze her expression. She scooped his son into her arms and buried her face in his hair as if he were medicine. "Tony," she said. "Tony, I'm so glad to see you."

"Isabel?" Ben had never seen her so upset. He dropped to his knees. "Come here." As he reached for her, Tony struggled to get to his supplies.

"Bob," his son called.

Isabel refused to lift her head—to look—or to let Ben hold her. He heard footsteps on the landing above.

"What has that woman done now?"

Isabel looked up at last and wrapped her arms around his shoulders. "I knew you'd be on my side."

From the landing Leah stared at Ben and Tony as if they were intruders. Ben stared back. He'd love a fight. He'd resented her on Will's behalf for years. For Isabel, he'd pretty much pitch the woman into the nearest dirty snowbank.

"I'm always on your side, Isabel." Locked on Leah's curious face, he made no effort to hide any of his confusing feelings for her. Let Leah jump to the worst conclusions she could imagine. Isabel needed to know she could trust a man to choose her first.

CHAPTER NINE

LEAH DECIDED to go to her hotel soon after Ben arrived. Isabel closed the door behind her former mother-in-law. "Thanks for coming, Ben. You must have heard my telepathic bleats for help."

He grinned. She'd never noticed the appeal of his self-conscious smile before, and she tried to resist it now. "I'd like to say I'm that powerful," he said, "but Tony couldn't wait to show you his latest SpongeBob haul."

She scooped up Tony, who was wrestling with his thermos, and reburied her face in his thick black hair. "I love this boy and his excellent taste," she said. "You're a lifesaver, Tony."

He peered at her. "Lipesaber," he said around the top of the thermos.

"Come with me." She swung him to the floor again. "We'll wash that and put some nice juice in it."

"Nice juice?" Ben asked behind her, his amusement as warm as a touch.

"Would I have any other kind?" She tried to look

nonchalant. "Really—I want to thank you for help-ing me fend off Leah. I half expected her to claim squatter's rights."

"She seemed happy enough to go after I told her it was snowing again." He got close enough to run his hand along Tony's arm. His fingers trailed over Isabel's shoulder, too. It might have been an acci-dent. It felt unaccountably good. "We should head home, too," Ben said. "Since the accident, I'm gun-shy about driving Tony in bad weather."

"Sure. I didn't think." She hurried into the kitchen and set Tony on the counter as she washed his thermos.

Ben leaned next to his son. "You're almost fin-ished. You'll have to hire a real-estate agent soon."

"Not really." She almost spilled her guts, but re-membered just in time that he'd be as hurt as she had been. "A guy came by today. Maybe he has his ear to the Goodwill donation truck routes. He arrived just after Leah, so I asked him to call me later."

"You can't just take some guy who wandered to your door. Selling this house is an investment."

She glanced at Tony, unwilling to argue in front of him, but she and Ben had to talk about this. She couldn't back down—for her nephew's sake. "This investment belongs to him, too."

Spending the day with Leah, she'd formed a hard shell or Ben's frown might have put her off.

"I've had enough today, Ben. Do what you want

with Tony's money, but I'm putting aside everything that belongs to him. If you won't take it, I'll
put it in an account under my name, but it'll be
easier to explain if you just accept it now and take
charge."

"Will made my wife care about him, when I
couldn't get through to her. I feel as if he stole my
son. Now you want to blackmail me into accepting
money from him?"

"Blackmail?" His accusation stung. "You could
choose a path that gives you options."

"Or you can turn him into a trust-fund baby."

"He is a trust-fund baby. If you want it to be from
his 'uncle,' I won't contradict you, but he's going to
wonder why I hold the purse strings rather than you."
She slicked her hair back only to have it spring into
her eyes again. "And I don't like arguing with you."

Ben considered, his mouth thin, his jaw sharp as
a knife. "This subject makes us harsh with each
other. Why don't we agree to talk about it sometime
before Tony turns eighteen?"

"I'll put it off for tonight, but we have to talk soon
so I can settle Will's estate."

"We'll talk." But he looked as if they'd do that on
a cold day in hell. He picked up Tony. "Drive carefully, Isabel. The roads may be slick."

"I'll see you at your house." She emphasized the
words, reassuring him that she'd avoid careening
into someone else or a light post.

After Ben and Tony left, she locked up, but still walked out to her car about the same time Ben finished storing Tony's SpongeBob bounty in the back of theirs. He leaned in to fasten Tony's car seat. Isabel waited, her engine idling in snowflakes that grew thicker by the minute.

With a brief nod, he started his car. She followed him home, driving in his tracks. When they parked at his house, she carried the day-care baggage while he cradled Tony, sleeping, in his arms.

"I shouldn't have let him fall asleep, but he's had a busy day." Barely above a whisper, Ben's husky tone made Isabel uneasy in her own skin.

He'd been her best friend. She'd worried about her own marriage, but hadn't looked elsewhere for comfort. Ben's voice shouldn't affect her at all. Still, shimmers of excitement made moments with him worth waiting for.

Isabel's mother met them at the door, relief written on her face. "I was worried. Oh, Tony's asleep." She dropped to a whisper. "Let me take him, Ben. You put your things away. I'll ease him awake, feed him and get him to bed."

"Amelia, you have to take a break. I know how to care for Tony, and I don't want you working yourself to the bone."

"I can't do enough for this little guy." Waking her grandson with the softest kiss, Amelia drew him out of his father's arms.

They were rebuilding their family. Isabel recognized the love in her mother's tone. It had comforted her all her life.

In return, she was hiding a dark secret about her sister. She trusted her parents to leave Tony with Ben, but they wouldn't appreciate being lied to any more than she or Ben had.

"Isabel?" Ben brought her back to the present. "Coming in out of the snow?"

She looked into his face, this man for whom she was lying to her mother and father. Lines around his eyes and mouth reminded her he was still grieving, still in shock himself. He raised both brows in a wordless inquiry tinged with a warning.

"Let me take the bags." He reached for Tony's shopping. His touch teased her through the heavy wool sleeve of her coat. His body seemed bigger, stronger, more forceful than she'd ever noticed.

"Maybe you should come with me," he said.

"You sound as if you're threatening me."

He shook his head. Shock chilled his expression. "I'd never do that."

She let the shopping bags go, afraid the blood pumping in her ears was loud enough for Ben to hear. She felt too close to him so she fled to her room.

"I'D LIKE TO VISIT the day care with you this morning, Ben. Leah phoned to say she's busy so I don't have to go to the house."

"School, Iz-bell." Tony kicked and Ben, still holding the laces on his boy's shoe, accidentally untied it. He looked up from his son fidgeting on the stairs. "Hold on, buddy."

"Ben?"

"I'm no threat today?"

"I'm sorry. I was tired and overreacting."

She still looked tired. Instead of her usual jeans, she'd put on a black skirt and a soft white sweater that emphasized her too-sharp collarbones and tied at her waist, which seemed more narrow.

"You're losing weight," he said.

"Maybe you should stop looking at me." She blushed, and he wrapped his hand around her leg, before thinking such a touch was too intimate. She stepped back. "How about it? Can I go with you?"

"Yeah." Ben finished tying Tony's shoe and let go, a rodeo rider, roping a calf. "Ready?"

"No." Tony started back up the stairs, hand-over-hand on the rail. "Get Bob."

"No Bob today, bud." Ben went after his son and turned him back down the stairs. Isabel pulled their coats from the closet.

Ben helped Tony on with his and then put on his own. He held the front door for Isabel. "Should we tell your parents we'll be out?"

She frowned, doing up her top button, and then took her phone out of her pocket.

"I'll help Tony into the car." He looked at her,

dialing. What had really passed between them last night? "Come on, Tony. Ready for school?"

Tony giggled with pure delight. Ben held his son close. Maybe too close, since Tony struggled to get down, but moments like this—the ones that felt too painfully sweet—reminded him of the phone call he'd had from the police.

Some officer had started with "There's been an accident..." By the time the man said Faith's name, Ben had fallen into his chair, as weak as any child. "Tony," he'd said. He'd tried with his wife, but his first thought that afternoon had been for the baby boy who owned him heart and soul.

"Dad-dee." Tony squirmed again, and Ben loosened his arms.

"Sorry." He kissed Tony's head, and coughed to clear a lump of relieved tears from his throat. "I love you, Son."

"Lub, Dad." Tony planted a wet kiss on Ben's cheek. Ben wore the moisture as a badge. He couldn't do without his son. Couldn't imagine surviving if he'd lost him.

Ben completed the process of installing Tony in the car as Isabel ran down the sidewalk. She scrambled into the seat beside him.

"All set. Mom's making Dad take her out for lunch."

He started the car and gave all his attention to pulling away from the curb. Last night stuck in his mind. He couldn't forget she'd suggested he was threatening her and then run for her life.

At the school, Isabel leaped out first. She must have knocked herself over the head last night, because she'd clearly had more sleep than he dreamed of having again.

"I'll get Tony." She climbed in the back and soon hauled him out. "Have you left him alone here yet?"

"No. I've only been with you and then with your mom. I stood in the back of the room while she cross-examined the teachers. Tony played with the other kids, but he'd look back at me for reassurance. I don't have the guts to leave him yet."

"He's probably vulnerable because of the accident. He's had play dates before."

"But Faith stayed for them." Mad as hell at Faith, he couldn't deny that Tony had loved her and she'd loved him. "She was a good mom."

"Yeah. She had a good example."

He couldn't dwell too long on Faith's finer points. "Here we are."

He held the door and Isabel carried Tony inside. Immediately, the boy kicked to get down. He loved playing with the other kids.

Mrs. Nash met them at her office. "Morning." She reached for Tony, who tiptoed for her to pick him up. "I saw you drive in. Mr. Jordan. We have the opening. The other family is planning to move as we expected, and Tony's welcome to start here on Monday if you'd both like."

"Thanks." Ben fought an urge to grab Tony and run. Single parents used day care every day—no doubt by the millions. "They want me back at work."

"I understand your ambivalence." Mrs. Nash might have been offended, but instead she offered compassion. "Why don't you let me take Tony into his classroom? You and Isabel can take a break. There's a coffee shop in the strip mall at the end of the block. We'll just see how the little fellow does for a half hour or so."

Ben put his hand on Isabel's shoulder. She distracted him, moving into his touch. "Are you sure he'll be all right?"

"Fine," Mrs. Nash said. "I have your cell number on the paperwork you filled out. Do you have your phone?"

He nodded with a lump in his throat as big as the cell. This day care was his first decision as a single parent. He'd just as soon not screw up Tony's life.

"I'm glad your family is so involved with Tony." Mrs. Nash smiled into his little boy's face. "Want to see the other children?" He nodded and she set him on the floor. "Say goodbye to Daddy."

"Bye." Tony waved and ran to the door of the room he usually visited. "Dad?"

Ben forced himself to speak over a massive knot. "See you in a little while, Son. Have fun."

Tony hesitated, but Mrs. Nash led him into the room. "You like puzzles, don't you, Tony?"

The door swung shut. Ben dragged his hand across his mouth.

"We had to let him try it out." Isabel took his elbow and led him toward the front door.

"We?" Ben asked.

She nodded. "We. I'm here, too. I'm part of the family."

What part? He'd like to know. "How about that coffee?"

"Sounds good. He went without much argument."

Ben smiled at the wet ground and hunched into his coat. "Makes a guy feel unnecessary."

"Not a chance."

He opened the passenger door for her and she climbed in.

"Wait, Ben."

He paused and she pressed both hands to the sides of his face, warming him in the frozen air. "I'm sorry."

"What happened last night?"

"I looked at you and my mom and Tony. You were a family—we're a family. I don't know why we can't tell her."

He broke away. "Are you planning to?"

"No. I promised and I won't without talking to you, but how do you think she and Dad are going to feel when they do find out?"

"If we're lucky, they never will."

"Not 'we' this time. I want the truth out. I'm afraid I'll slip. I'm afraid Mom and Dad will be angry we've lied and they'll want revenge." She nodded at him. "Just as we want Will and Faith paid back."

He'd like to deny he wanted his ex-wife to suffer, even though she was beyond pain now. Half of trying to get over this mess was his frustration, because Faith and Will might have died, but they'd also had the last word.

"I want to know why they cheated on us," he said. "I don't want them hurt."

"And you didn't want to hurt me last night? You were just afraid I might tell my mom something she's entitled to know."

"What's changed? You chose Tony and me when we started this."

"I was stunned then. I hadn't seen my father looking like a walking ghost. My mother hadn't asked me over and over where Faith was going with her suitcases."

"I'm asking you to help me keep my son."

"You've changed, too," she said, losing her temper.

"I'm supposed to be the angry one. You came down this morning perfectly happy."

"I was pretending, okay?" She tried to turn away on the seat, but he caught her legs. "I tell myself if I pretend you and I haven't changed, I'll start to believe it," she said.

"I don't feel guilty for wanting you."

A sigh hissed between her lips. She looked young and frightened and aroused with her mouth slightly open, her lips full and red from the cold.

He didn't stop to think. He kissed her, tilting her head so he could reach her throat and the tender flesh beneath her chin. She shuddered and her fingers flexed into his nape.

"Isabel." He whispered her name, because he liked saying it. When he said it, she seemed to fill his head.

"The school," she said.

"On the other side of the car." But he kissed the lobe of her ear, suckling for a sweet moment as she fell against him and he was grateful. She wanted him as much as he wanted her. "All the same…"

"THIS TIME you're the one with second thoughts."

Ben turned, pastry dough drying in his hands. "You're everywhere, Isabel." For the first time since she'd come back to Hartsfield, he wasn't pleased to see her.

They'd shared a coffee he'd never remember and returned to the school close as two people who knew they'd eventually make love.

At least he knew.

Isabel's soft laugh worked like the caress of her

fingers. He had to concentrate to understand what she said.

"Most men don't bake when they think they might be seducing the wrong woman."

Over his shoulder, he met her challenging gaze. Dust and all, she seemed to glow in the dusky orange of a sunset without snow. "You're disputing my manhood?" His voice had gone deep. He was tense from head to toe. He wanted Isabel in so many ways. Her body seemed to come alive the second he touched her. She was so easy to be with. She loved his son. She loved family. "It may sound old-fashioned, but I can prove anything you'd like to question."

She backed down immediately, her gaze skittering away. Even her flushed skin enticed him. He needed to feel her, pliant and clinging, with no thought for why they shouldn't be together.

"Baklava?" she asked, with a nod to the pastry on his counter.

"Coward." She'd changed the subject.

"Maybe I am." She nudged the flour canister. "You started making that because it was Faith's favorite."

"We made it together."

"To patch up after arguments without having to actually say you were sorry."

He returned to his task. "You do know too much about me. She used this to make up, too."

"Maybe if you'd talked instead of baking together…"

"You'd still be with Will?"

"No." Her quick denial relieved his unexpected jealousy. She opened the fridge and took out a bottle of water. "He'd have found someone else. When you spend solitary days packing and cleaning a house, you have plenty of time to think—and I think I bored him."

"He was an idiot."

"He never baked."

That did it. He dropped the pastry and walked across the kitchen. "I am a man, Isabel." She closed her eyes before he touched her. He studied her softly angled face as he slid his hands down her back, indulging in the infinite pleasure of her curves against him. He held her with the hunger of a man who'd never eaten.

Warm and soft and firm where her body gave him the most pleasure, she arched against the pressure of his palms. He took her mouth. For now she belonged to him. He'd erase any other man's touch.

She started to resist, keeping her mouth closed. He cradled her face, pressed his thumbs against her lips, rubbing gently. "Open your mouth, Isabel."

She opened her eyes instead. Her steady stare refused him until he stroked her lips again, and her eyes narrowed. Her face crumpled as if she might cry.

"Damn." He let her go. Memories of Faith and the rejections he'd never understood powered him away from Isabel.

"Wait." Her hand on his back, affection and need in her tone, stopped him.

He faced her again. "I'm not playing a game."

"I'm afraid," she said. "I don't want to be abandoned again."

"I can't promise anything." Except that he'd likely never be in the same room and not want her in his arms.

"I need the promises." She held his hands, asking for his consideration. "The ones Will made and broke."

He pulled away. "I won't touch you with his name on your mouth."

She looped her arms around his neck, ignoring his aloofness. "You want Will and Faith to disappear— as if they never existed. We can't forget them. They're part of our lives, and they're vital to Tony's, but we're still so close to them I don't trust what you feel."

"Knowing all that, I can't promise." Ben held her waist. "I never thought of you like this before. Now I can't seem to stop, but trust is something I'm not sure I'll ever feel again."

"Not even for me?"

"I can't even talk to you without hurting your feelings."

He took her in his arms as if he had a right. She opened her mouth this time and kissed him back with frank need that shook him. Rational thought fled. He lifted her onto the cold granite island. The better to feel her breasts pushing against his chest, taste her breath as hot as his own. Even her delicate muscles seemed to flex against his palms.

Staring into her eyes, he pushed his hands beneath her thighs and ran his fingers down the legs of her jeans, enjoying every sinew that tightened in anticipation of his touch. When he pulled her legs around his waist, she scooted closer. She held his face with more possession and passion than he'd ever known. She brushed his lips once, twice, until he couldn't stand any more teasing and held her head to deepen the kiss.

He mattered to Isabel. God help him, he should have realized he'd stopped mattering to Faith, because she'd never touched him like this.

He nudged Isabel closer still. The instant she felt his arousal, she arched, and he almost laughed with joy. He only held back because she might not understand. Smiling, he kissed her cheek and the hollow of her ear. He opened his mouth against her throat, his smile fading as her moan hummed against his lips.

"Someone will find us," she said, taut with passion.

"Let's go to my room."

"I can't." She devoured his mouth, rousing him until reaching some room, somewhere, became imperative. "There's the past we haven't dealt with, and the truth."

He lifted his head, losing all connection with sanity. "Blackmail?"

"No." She said it against his lips. "I've never made love with a man without being sure it was right."

"I've never felt more right, but we can't stay here."

She tightened her calves and he groaned. No choice but to bury his face in the hollow of her shoulder and ease his pain in the cradle of her legs.

"Stop," she said, though need pulsed in her voice.

He tried to do as she'd asked, though he ached to thrust against her one more time. He pulled away, reaching for the counter at his back. She looked stunned and vulnerable, and he wanted to tear off her inconvenient clothes and finish what they'd started.

"You should go," he said.

"Are you angry?"

Surprised, he jerked his head back. "What?"

She glanced around the room, somehow including the whole house in her nod. "Because we might be disturbed."

"Are you nuts? I am a man. I understand *no*."

"I know you're a man. Your baking is all over my sweater."

He took one step toward her before she slid off the island.

"No." She held up both trembling hands. Regret pinched her face. "We'll end up making love right here if you prove anything else."

Nowhere near satisfied, he let her weave out of the

room. Her unsteady gait seduced him. He would have followed, but he suspected he'd fall flat on his face. His head understood *no*. His body didn't have a clue.

TALK ABOUT MISTAKES. She'd nearly made her worst one yet. Making love with Ben couldn't solve any problems. Her parents would never understand.

In the middle of the night, Isabel packed her things. She'd stayed to be with Tony, but each new moment under this roof taunted her with the fact that Ben was becoming a necessity.

In the morning, she knocked on his door before Tony was awake. He opened it right away. He looked so glad to see her his smile hurt.

Then he pulled her inside, and his slightest touch felt delicious. She could hardly speak when he put his arms around her. She leaned away from him. "We shouldn't. You and Tony are closer than ever to my mom and dad, and they'd be appalled at the idea of you and me together."

A vee formed between his eyebrows. "We've been starved for the feelings we give each other."

"You can't say that." Nor could she let herself agree. "It may be just how Faith and Will rationalized their affair."

"If it is, they said it in bed."

"But you and I are not people who leap before looking. I'm not feeling as righteous as I was about them."

"We've done nothing wrong, Isabel."

She looked at him, loving the boxers that rode low on his hips and just right on his thighs, a T-shirt that hugged his muscled chest. There was plenty she wanted to do and feel, wrong or right.

"We're alone. We're adults." He surprised her, swinging her close enough to brush his thighs, pressing his lips to the side of her neck, just where his kiss triggered goose bumps that chased up and down her arms and legs. "I want you. You want me."

"You were married to my sister. She and Will haven't been gone long." She pushed out of his arms and turned away.

"And your parents?"

"It's all the same problem. I want to wrap your arms around me and tell you everything that's bothering me, but you're not just my best friend anymore. I don't know how to deal with what I feel for you now."

"I won't give up on you—on us—and I'm willing to face your parents' disapproval if we have to."

She knew he was close before he touched her. He linked his hands at her waist and pulled her against him. Being in his arms was such a relief—that couldn't last. "I packed my stuff last night."

His chin brushed her hair as he turned his head. "It's still last night. Why would you want to leave Tony and me?"

With his lips at her ear, she couldn't remember, and she certainly didn't want to go. "I told you."

He leaned so far around her he reached the corner of her mouth. She needed more. She turned and spread her fingers across his chest, pleased to find his racing heartbeat and tight nipples.

"Don't tease, Isabel."

He kissed her and she clung, craving him as if they'd barely been apart for a second. At last, he raised his head and she buried her face in the hollow of his throat, breathing in his musky, irresistible scent. "Maybe with some space we'll be rational enough to work it all out."

"I like you in my face."

"I still have to go until being with you feels at least as right as it does wrong."

His hands traced her back and sides, sending shudders through her. His arousal, pressed to the pit of her belly, made her feel womanly and strong and needed. For these moments, she was Ben's and he was hers, but last night's regrets would come back. She shook her head.

"Don't go." He traced her hairline with his mouth. "Do you want me to say please?"

"I want to belong, and I never will here. I'm your friend's wife, your wife's sister. And I want you in my bed."

"Where I need you to be. Urgently."

She walked to his door, feeling as if she were climbing hand-over-hand up a slim rope. "I'll come back tonight to see Tony, but then I have to go home."

"You don't want to stay in that house."

"No." She didn't bother to lie. "But I'm too con-fused to stay here, and we're bound to do something that gives us away." She turned the doorknob with so much force she hurt her hand.

Then she went back to her room and got her bags. As she ran down the stairs, she looked back, half hoping Ben would stop her. He didn't. Even he could see she was right.

Tears filled her eyes. Being desired felt intense, addictive, precious. She'd struggled not to cry over Faith and Will, feeling foolish and betrayed, trying to find her pride. As she left Ben's house, the tears streamed down her cheeks. Even crying felt good.

CHAPTER TEN

ON TONY'S FIRST morning of day care, Isabel linked arms with her mother and gritted her teeth at the open window that looked into the little boy's classroom. Her heart broke with strange, tender loss and with pride at Tony's lack of fear. Fortunately, because of his visits, he just wanted to play.

In his favorite spot, the art center, he smeared purple paint on a blank sheet of paper. Ben turned from his son, shrugging at Isabel and her parents.

He came to them, entirely ignored by Tony. George was already ushering Amelia toward the front. Ben wrapped an arm around Isabel and said, "You look angry."

"No, strangely sad. He's growing up. Why does that hurt so much?"

"Because time goes too fast. Be careful, though. If Tony sees you, he may think he's supposed to cry. He's nineteen months old, and we have plenty of firsts to get through still."

"You're happy for a guy who was so uncertain

yesterday." Forgetting caution, she grabbed his lapel.

"I'm glad he's happy. What's to cry about?"

Isabel opened her hand. "Are you working all day today?"

"Probably not. I miss him already. I got used to having him around."

"Will you come by the house before you pick him up? I'd love to come, too." She nodded at her parents, already waiting on the sidewalk in the cold.

"What about Leah? Isn't she going home today?"

Her mother-in-law had calmed some. She had still wanted to inspect each box Isabel packed, but she'd broken away early the night before to talk to Ray about Will's estate. "She's starting back this morning. She doesn't like to drive in the dark." Then Isabel remembered the Realtor. "But Mr. Lofton has papers for me to sign so he can put the house on the market. Maybe you could call me before you come back."

Her mother and father, beside Ben's car, heard the last. "You've hired a Realtor?" her mother asked. "Why didn't you say?"

"I've been busy at the house. I don't want to think about it by the time I see you all."

"What are you planning to do after you sell?" her dad asked. "Are you going back to Middleburg?"

She avoided Ben. "I'm up in the air. I had a job in Middleburg, but they called a couple of days ago and needed a firm date for my return. I couldn't give them that so I'm unemployed again."

"That's not right," her mother said.

"It is, but I appreciate your outrage, Mom. I'm going to look for a job here. I always loved this place, and I've been thinking about a town house in D.C."

"I'm glad you'll still be close to Tony." Her mother's smile looked inward. "Your father and I should think of going home soon, but I've enjoyed spending so much time with the baby. Ben, let's try to stay this close."

Isabel watched him. Would he be grateful for a stronger family, or would he resist her mother's attachment to his son?

"I hope you'll all come when you can, and I'll bring Tony up more often. He needs all of us."

For the first time, Isabel thought there might be a chance he'd agree to tell the truth. Behind her, the clock on the peaked roof chimed the hour. "I have to go if I want to leave early."

"We'll see you at dinner." Isabel's mother walked backward on the wide, pale sidewalk. She reversed to take her husband's arm. "We'll celebrate Tony's first school day."

That was what Tony called it—school. At less than two years old, he had a child's eagerness to "be big" fast.

"Don't forget to keep your cell phone with you," Ben said.

She looked at him, unable to say all that burned inside her. That she only wanted to be with him and Tony, that everything else, job, future, freedom, had begun to seem less vital. "Okay. I'll see you later. Can I bring anything, Mom?"

"Just yourself."

Isabel waved at them, her mouth too tight to say goodbye. She got in her car, feeling as naked as the winter trees. This was her family, and she stood between Ben and her parents, guarding a secret that could destroy them all. Its weight grew each day.

Leah was waiting in her car when Isabel drove up. She climbed out and walked up the steps at Isabel's side. "I guess today is goodbye."

"Not forever, Leah. We'll stay in touch."

"I met with Ray Paine."

"Good." Isabel unlocked the door and let her in. The house, dressed with only Isabel's things, felt more welcoming. Before this morning, she'd walked in each day and sensed only the lack of love this home had borne like a wound.

"I won't stay long, but I wanted to thank you." Her voice broke. "Ray told me how generous you've been with both Tony and me. More than I deserved." Leah shut the door at their backs. "I know I've been—obnoxious, but I tend to panic and say crazy things when I'm upset. I hit back before I know whether I should."

Isabel hugged Leah, hoping the worst was over. "If I lost a son, maybe I'd be the same."

"Thanks, Isabel," Leah said through tears. She stepped back and shrugged out of her coat. "I wish I'd seen Tony. He obviously means more to you than I understood, and I think he must have mattered as much to my son."

"He did." Isabel thought of Will without rancor for the first time. She'd never doubted his love for Tony. "He would have provided everything I have for—our nephew—if he'd ever thought he might die so young."

"I didn't know my son at all, and now it's too late." Leah seemed unaware she'd begun to cry. "And I've treated you horribly since I've been here." She pulled a handkerchief out of nowhere and blew her nose. "Ignore me. I'll make us some coffee before I go. After I saw Ray, I couldn't leave with all my bad behavior between us."

Isabel hung their coats before she followed her former mother-in-law to the kitchen. "Do you think the house looks right?"

"You'll be lucky if you find another place before you sell." Leah had already placed a filter in the coffeemaker, and she was spooning in coffee. "Will you miss this house?"

"I thought so for a second when we came in, but it stopped being a happy place a long time ago."

"I understand."

"Leah, you've been struck by lightning."

She turned from the counter, smoothing her hands along her sedate black neck-to-calf dress. "Don't count on the new me lasting. But I am ashamed I treated you as if you were a thief."

She always had, really. She'd thought Isabel had stolen her son. Isabel nodded, unwilling to pretend Leah's accusations hadn't hurt, but she could forgive, too.

"I really don't want to lose touch with you, Isabel. I'm sure I'll get a little crazy and blame everything on you again, but deep down, I care, and I'd love to know I can talk to you about Will from time to time." She smiled, running her multiringed hand over her face. "We can talk about you, too."

Isabel weakened. "Maybe we'll always rub each other like sandpaper, but I don't want to lose you, either."

"A sandpaper relationship's not bad. It'll keep us on our toes." She glanced at her watch. "I'd better move."

They shared a cup of coffee and parted, declaring a truce.

"Have a safe trip. Call my cell when you get home."

"I will."

Isabel waved until she couldn't see Leah anymore. Then she went back inside and put finishing touches on the house in preparation for Neal Lofton's visit.

He came late that afternoon. Isabel had to tell Ben she couldn't meet him to pick up Tony, and she felt cheated. She signed Lofton's contracts, and he plunged a For Sale sign into her lawn, assuring her the house would go so fast she'd wonder where she would live.

She already did.

She returned to Ben's house for dinner that night. He asked her if she'd ducked him. Even in small ways they had a lot to learn about trust.

All the nights after, she visited Tony, but she avoided Ben. Between longing for him, missing her nephew and each night getting more caught up in her newly complex family, Isabel found staying at her own home difficult.

Three weeks after Tony started day care, Amelia called. "Morning, sweetie—I hope I didn't wake you."

Isabel had already made coffee, read the newspaper and cleaned the house to make it fit for a prospective buyer's viewing pleasure. These nights she found sleep elusive. Too many thoughts got in the way.

"I've been up awhile, Mom. Are you at Ben's?"

"I came to make my cinnamon rolls for Tony."

"Mmm, I wish I'd known. Everything okay over there?"

"Sure. I'm just calling to remind you about Tony's recital tonight."

The Children's Cottage featured a music teacher who'd put together a program for the children. They were singing at a nearby community center as all the parents and friends of the children wouldn't fit into their building. Isabel had fended off invites to the event. Even when she heard Tony practicing, she'd blubbered like a baby.

The poignancy of his big-boy efforts twisted her in knots. She couldn't help being sorry that Faith would never see her boy singing his song

"Isabel, are you still there?"

"I'm not sure about tonight."

"Yes, you are. Tony's growing up. You'll be sorry if you miss even one step he takes along the way."

"That's the nail on the head." And a total relief to admit it out loud.

"You'll never lose him. We may have been complacent about seeing him before, but that's changed. We've all learned how unreliable life can be."

Isabel's heart cracked in several places. "I'll be there." She was foolish to spend more time with Ben when she couldn't have him in her life, but her mother would get around to questioning her real motives if she kept staying away.

"It starts at seven, Mom?"

"But Ben has to take Tony over at six-thirty."

"Okay. See you there."

"The school's putting on a little party afterward."

"And the whole family's invited?"

"Seems to me you visit Tony, but you're trying to stay away from the rest of us lately."

Her mother's throwaway remark was just what she'd dreaded. Isabel got off the phone before her mom slipped into interrogation mode.

For the rest of the day she worked on spinning her volunteer work into a reputable résumé and then called several headhunters. Surprised at how much credit they were willing to give the fund-raisers she'd organized, she agreed to an interview the next day.

She finally turned off the computer and stood, stretching as she scoured the dark blue sky outside the office window. More snow. Or maybe a thunderstorm. It didn't look good, but she liked the excitement of violent weather.

Isabel showered and put on a white wool skirt and a pale blue cashmere cardigan, barely buttoned to the top of her translucent blue bra.

Against her better judgment, she wanted to look good for Ben. She examined herself in the mirror and saw someone different, someone more willing to put herself at risk. Considering it might be temporary daring on her part, she thought about changing but grabbed her keys and coat. The bell rang as she reached for the door.

She wasn't surprised to find Ben. She'd wanted to see him so badly it was as if she'd summoned him.

"Hey." His gaze was all male, all appreciation, and he started a flutter of pleasant anticipation inside her. So much for days of trying to be sensible. "I had to take Tony over early and then they threw all the parents out for distracting the children."

She pushed her fingers through her hair, aware that newly washed, it was shiny and full of life. "How did you distract the kids?"

Interest darkened his eyes. "Mrs. Carter tried to put them through their paces, but they were more interested in us."

"So you came here." She was glad and she couldn't hide her relief.

With a laugh that was pure foreplay, Ben took her chin in one hand and kissed her, teasing, touching, tasting. She put her arms around him, holding tight.

"You've been avoiding me," he said, "even in my own house." Then he pressed his open mouth to her throat. The gentle pull of his kiss robbed her of thought and speech.

She had to learn each line and plane of his face. He hadn't shaved since morning, but she liked the friction of his stubble.

"Answer me," he said, his hands restless on her back.

"I am." She followed the outline of his ear with her lips. His breath escaped in a heady moan, and he slid his hands beneath the hem of her sweater. She could hardly believe she was touching him, but she couldn't stop.

"Soft." The word sounded odd in the unfamiliar tone of his need.

She loosened his tie and then his collar, desperate to touch him, too. "Ben?"

"I can't tell which is softer, this sweater or your skin." He splayed his hands across her back, making her feel small, delicate. At the same time, he lowered his head to the vee her sweater's open buttons made above her breasts.

His mouth there should feel wrong. It didn't. He opened a button.

She looked down. Her bra hid nothing. She looked at Ben, whose hungry glance seemed to touch her face as well as her breasts.

"More." Her own voice, pleading, shocked her.

"I wish." Peeling the fragile material of her bra back with one finger, he suckled her flesh. "We have to stop."

But stopping didn't seem to be on his mind. He traced both breasts with tender, trembling fingertips until she was arching into his hands.

Ben's shoulder muscles bunched beneath his shirt. Frustration made her groan when, as she reached for his tie again, he caught her hands. "Later." He stared into her eyes, and his were too dark to read.

He looked doubtful, as if he knew they should go, but he couldn't. She wanted to laugh as he kissed her, but holding him, touching him, was too serious. She felt alive. Full of life. "When, later?"

His smile went straight to her head. "Whenever you ask."

"I'm asking." They both knew she'd beg again.

"I'm afraid you'll change your mind when you see your parents."

She stiffened. Not only would they be appalled that she could make love with Ben, they'd believe she was taking him from Faith. "You might be right. I've tried to stop wanting you, but the second I saw you I changed my mind."

He returned to her breast and immediately erased every other human being from her mind. "I won't let you push me away again."

"Don't sound possessive."

He looked at her, his lips moist, forbidden. "You make me feel possessive."

Tension poured into the silence between them. "Why did you have to talk?" Easing away, Isabel re-buttoned her sweater. Ben tried to smooth his hair with his hands, but she'd mussed it so well she had to help him. "Do I look like you?"

His lips thinned. "How do I look?"

"As if I've been trying to tear your hair out."

"You didn't pull." Half a smile relaxed his face. "Why have you been so distant lately?"

"I don't want to hurt anyone. I keep thinking of Will and Faith. Did they feel like this?"

"You and I are not married. Will and Faith should have divorced us both before they started sleeping to-gether. They cheated. We are not cheating on them now." He adjusted the knot of his tie, which she'd twisted. "And don't accuse me of trying to pay them back, because I never thought once about them. I think about you nearly twenty-four disturbing hours a day. Every time you walk into my house and look at me with that careful, detached expression, I want to make you whimper with the hunger that won't let me sleep at night."

She could hardly hear over the beating of her own heart. "You know how you always say I can't hide my feelings? When I look at you I want your hands on me. I want to touch you." She closed her eyes, still aroused by his hands. "I dream of you at night, Ben, if I sleep at all."

"Let's do something about it." He stroked the curve of her throat.

Her body was painfully sensitive. "I can't. How would we explain an affair to my parents? And besides, I had a plan. Whether I mean to or not, I keep letting you get in my way."

"What's your plan?" He twined his fingers with hers. "Tell me."

She'd adapted her behavior to Will's moods for years. When he got angry, she'd grown anxious, but she didn't fear the faint glitter in Ben's eyes. "I faxed out my résumé, and I have a job interview."

His genuine smile made her feel better at once. Ben was pleased for her. "Where? Are you looking forward to it?"

"Yeah—and how many people look forward to a

job interview? I should be scared. My skills seem sparse, but I'm going to convince an advertising agency that I'm good enough to hire."

"For?"

"Writing copy."

"Sort of like lying for the company cause, huh?"

She grinned. "I hate it in my personal life, but I'm aching for a chance to do it for a living."

"Come on." He helped her put on her coat. "We have to go, or we'll miss the start."

He took her hand as they walked down the porch steps. Immediately, she thought, what if someone sees us? Who could, in the darkness outside her house? And why shouldn't she lean into Ben's shoulder? For these few moments, they were a man and woman, on the verge of an emotional commitment. Bad marriages had denied them loyalty they could believe in until neither knew how to accept love anymore. Ben seemed as astonished as she that someone else could need him.

Nevertheless, when he started the car, she turned to him. "I have to ask you something."

"Not tonight, Isabel." He glanced at her, his face in shadows. "Not when all I can think is how much I want you back in my arms."

"I want that, too, but listen to me."

"Come on, Isabel."

"Ben, when you're watching Tony tonight, take a look at my mom and dad. See if you don't find lying hard."

"Tony's my son. George and Amelia are part of our family, but Tony is *my* son."

"Okay." In the back of her mind lay the knowledge that a court might look even more unfavorably on Ben when he admitted he'd hidden the truth to keep her parents from taking Tony. She'd known since before Will and Faith's accident, and she wanted to speak up, but she couldn't choose her parents over Ben or Ben over them.

They left the car at the community center. Isabel walked fast, distracted by her misgivings. Ben caught up with her and put his arm around her shoulders. "Come on, Iz-bell. Be my friend."

"Don't 'Iz-bell' me." But she smiled back as she put her arm around his waist.

"Hold on to me."

"Everything's changed," she said.

"I know." He leaned his cheek against her hair. "Sorry."

"Are you?" She looked up, needing the familiarity of his features. Instead, she saw a new man, even stronger than she'd known him, sexy and generous.

"No." He searched the trickle of people also headed for the building. "I'm glad I can feel this way about anyone. I'm a little startled it's you who makes me feel it, but I'm lucky, too. You're my best friend, and yet I want you more than I've ever wanted any woman in my life."

He said it simply. Words like those should have

some sort of accompaniment—music, cannons. She lifted her face, searching for the sky beyond the waving, clawlike branches and clouds scudding across a sliver of moon. Maybe a February storm would do.

She tried to pull away, but Ben wouldn't let her go. He didn't demand an answer, but he wouldn't free her, either.

TEN SECONDS into Tony's song, Ben understood what Isabel had been trying to tell him. The small class of toddlers belted out their number, each at a separate tempo. They all seemed to think they were performing dance solos, too. Through laughter, he fought off tears. Tony had both small hands wrapped around his father's soul.

He looked at Amelia beside him and George, just beyond. Amelia cried without noticing, and George sniffed so hard he could barely hold up his head.

They loved Tony, too. As much as he did?

No.

He'd draped his overcoat across his lap. Startling him, Isabel's hand slid onto his thigh. She refused to look at him, but when he put his hand beneath the coat, too, she let him link their fingers. She held on tight. She, who kept trying to push him away.

How could he tell the Deavers the truth? How could Isabel expect him to tell them? A father naturally loved his son more than anyone else could.

But George and Amelia, missing their older

daughter, brittle as two shells washed up on a beach—maybe they deserved better.

He'd deserved better. And so had the fierce, lovable and loving woman at his side.

What the hell was he supposed to do?

"He's wonderful, Ben." Amelia leaned into his shoulder. "I may be partial, but I believe he's the handsomest boy up there. He looks so much like Faith."

Bitterness hit Ben. "I think I'm in him, too," he said, his first outright lie.

He looked more closely at his son. Restlessness had dulled Faith's green eyes. Life gleamed from Tony. Happiness Ben wasn't sure he'd ever known, which only fortified his determination to cherish his son and keep him safe.

He leaned toward Isabel. "You're right, but I can't help it. Look at him and tell me you could do it."

"I can't." Unshed tears soaked her voice.

If only they were alone.

That thought repeated in his head as the children from the other classes sang and he and Isabel held hands beneath his coat like teenagers. It blared as if he were hearing the words out loud as the family shared the after-event snack of fruit juice and cookies.

He thought only about being alone with Isabel as he watched Amelia hug her with maternal affection that wrenched his heart out and threw it to the ground beside his car.

"I'm so glad you came," Amelia said. "You'd have been sorry to miss his first school show."

Isabel's lips trembled.

If only he could be alone with her.

"Night, Iz-bell." Tony lifted his arms and Isabel hugged him so hard she probably snapped a couple of ribs. He only giggled and hugged back.

"I'm coming with you, nut," she said, and then went back to her mother. "Night. Thanks for keeping after me about this."

Ben ducked inside the car to help Tony. By the time he climbed out to say good-night to Amelia and George, Isabel was heading to the passenger side, wiping her eyes so her mascara wouldn't run.

"I worry about her," Amelia said, low-voiced. "She's pining for something. I guess it's Will and Faith."

"I guess," Ben said. His second lie. "But she'll get better."

"With time." George surprised Ben with a shot of philosophy. He took his wife's arm. "Let's get back to the condo, honey. Time I put my feet up, and Tony needs his sleep."

They called good-nights over the rushing wind and the sprinkles of rain that had begun to pelt the pavement like thumbtacks thrown to the ground.

Tony fell asleep as soon as Ben started the car. Isabel turned so she could look at him. She didn't say anything, but Ben sensed her uncertainty. At her house, she leaned across the seat for a quick kiss that set the blood pounding in his temples. He couldn't even answer her whispered good-night.

Tony slept on as they reached home. He didn't wake as Ben hummed the song his son had chanted all over the house for the past two weeks. Ben changed him into pajamas and tucked him into bed.

Afterward, he washed the leftover dinner dishes and started a load of laundry. He put newspapers in the recycling bin and then wandered his house, too restless to sit, too anxious about Isabel to think about the late news or the book he'd started a few days ago.

If only they could be alone for an hour or two.

While he drank milk from the carton in the fridge, he stared at the list of names Faith had put on the door. She'd allowed no other clutter in her house, but she'd posted a list of emergency numbers and babysitters.

Including the college girl who'd watched Tony overnight when he and Faith had gone out of town. They hadn't used her for a year or more. She might be out of college. She might not babysit anymore.

She lived a few houses down the street.

He dialed her number.

She was in her last year. She still babysat, and she understood a single Dad's sudden need to leave his house. She assumed he had an unexpected overnight business trip. He didn't explain, but when she arrived with a canvas bag over her shoulder, he gave her his cell number and insisted she call if Tony needed him at all.

Then he thought twice, three times, ten times before he pulled away from his house. Need—absolute longing for Isabel—overcame common sense. He drove through lightning and pounding rain without calling to warn her he was on his way.

Rain soaked him as he got out of the car. He ran up the porch steps and rang her doorbell before he reminded himself his son should be his only priority. He had no time to think about any woman, even Isabel.

She opened the door. Rather, the wind blew it open in her hands. Rain rushed inside.

"Ben, where's Tony?"

"At home, with an all-night sitter." He stepped inside and shut the door to drip on her floor. "Come with me."

She glanced down at her flared thermal pajama pants and a thin-strapped top that hugged her lush, round breasts. "Where?"

"Anywhere but here or my house. Anywhere you never spent a night with Will."

She looked shocked. She hadn't been asleep. A woman didn't achieve her hollow cheeks and dark-circled eyes on regular sleep.

And still she was too beautiful to believe. He'd held her, kissed her, but he wanted her more with every passing moment.

"Come, Isabel."

"What would it mean?" Her challenge surprised him. He hadn't been sure she'd consider staying with him.

"I don't know," he said. "Maybe you'll just let me hold you, but if I don't share a night with you I may lose my mind."

"Tony's all right for the whole night?"

He only looked at her. As if he'd leave his son in danger.

"I don't know what to do."

"What do you want to do?" he asked.

She rubbed her face with her hands and then clasped them in front of her. No smile. She was obviously no more sure than he that staying together tonight would be right. "There is a place."

"Where you and Will didn't go?"

"Where Will refused to go."

At last he couldn't help smiling. She understood. "Perfect."

"I'll change clothes."

"Just get your coat. I'm fine with what you have on."

"You won't be in the morning when you have to look at this ensemble across a breakfast table." She started up the stairs. "I'll call while I pack."

"Call who?" he asked, following her.

"A friend from several of my committees owns a B and B just over the Maryland line. She won't ask questions, and she told me once they keep one room open for just-in-case."

"In case what?" He stopped at the main bedroom, but she continued to the door at the end of the hall. "Where are you going?"

"I sleep in here," she said.

"Good." She no longer slept in the bed she'd shared with Will, and he was glad. As glad as a barbarian whose woman had chosen him.

CHAPTER ELEVEN

"WHERE DID YOU TELL the sitter you were going?" Isabel asked as the storm buffeted his car.

"I didn't. She has my cell phone number." Maybe he should have had her test his phone.

"What if Amelia or George calls?"

"This late at night? You're looking for reasons to back out."

"Oh, yeah. I guess they might offer me a reason or two."

"You want me to take you home, Isabel?"

Silence. Then, "No."

She sounded startled. A little stunned himself, he gave her time to let the truth sink in. But that test phone call weighed on his mind. He'd never been Tony's single parent before. He worried for two. "Would you call my cell?"

"Huh?"

"Just to make sure it's working."

Laughing, she dug her own phone out of her purse. "I lo— Like a good dad."

He ignored her stumble. Once "I love you" had

gone without saying. Now those words had changed for them. His phone rang. "Thanks." He hit the talk button and then hit End. "Are you nervous, Isabel?"

"Nearly terrified."

Her confession eased the knot in his gut. "I'm glad I'm not the only one."

"We don't have to go through with it. We can still turn around."

He didn't even slow down as they approached the interstate ramp. "Where to?" If she wanted him to take her back, he would.

After the barest second, she pointed at the big green sign above the exit lane. "Fletcher's Crossing."

Both relieved and yet concerned they were making an unforgivable mistake, he turned down the ramp. He glanced at her, but for once, he couldn't catch a glimpse of her thoughts.

She occupied all his. Tonight made him feel responsible. Will had broken her trust. After Faith, he'd thought he might never risk being with anyone he could love again. But Isabel had told him they would both trust. She wanted the family Will had denied her.

Ben's mouth went dry. If he was wrong about his growing feelings for Isabel, he could hurt the woman who mattered most in his life.

"You're the one who looks as if you'd like to turn back, Ben."

"We've come too far. What time do you have to be in D.C. tomorrow?"

"Two-fifteen."

That took care of small talk until Isabel pointed to a sign that looked like a bouquet of trees wrapped in flowered ribbon.

"Not too manly," he said. Tension made him feel like a coward.

"I've stayed here before. The amenities make up for the frills."

"Amenities?"

"A whirlpool tub for two in every room." She stopped on a short breath as if she hadn't meant to sound so pleased.

He gripped the steering wheel. How did a man drive a roller coaster? "I shouldn't take that as an invitation?"

"I've always soaked with a book." She crossed her arms. "It might have been more responsible to bring a library tonight."

He parked in front of a wide, quaint porch. "You won't need a single volume."

Her laughter felt as warm as water. She didn't wait for him to open her door. They both got out and met, running up the steps.

Inside, the proprietor, Cleo Murphy, greeted Isabel with unfeigned affection, but then eyed him with mistrust. He didn't blame her, but he smiled, hoping to assure her he wouldn't harm Isabel.

"Are your bags in the car?" Cleo asked. "I'll have them brought up." She handed Isabel a key. "Your favorite room is open. We hardly have any guests. Call in the morning when you want breakfast."

Ben followed Isabel up the thick-carpeted stairs and into the room she opened. She stood aside, looking anxious again as the plank floor creaked beneath their feet.

"Don't be afraid," he said.

She lifted her head in a less-than-sanguine nod.

A massive four-poster dominated the room. Flowers dripped from the wallpaper. He scratched his arm. He sure didn't fit the setting. He was tempted to open the window and let in some air a man could breathe. But the room probably had less to do with the constriction in his chest than Isabel, close enough to touch, with no one to interrupt them.

"Excuse me," said a voice behind them.

Ben turned to let in a college kid. The boy set their small bags on a bench in front of the bed. Ben dug loose bills out of his pocket to tip the kid. The boy looked so surprised Ben had to wonder what kind of folding money he'd handed over.

"Good night." The kid pulled the key out of the lock and set it on a dresser next to the door. "Call the desk if you need anything."

The second the door shut, Isabel giggled. "You must have set up his college fund."

"Yeah." He gave the window a last, longing

look. "Does Cleo know you well enough to know about Will?"

"She knows we'd split. And she was never Will's biggest fan. Like I said, he refused to come here." She unbuttoned her coat and hung it in the closet.

Then she came back and started on his shirt buttons as if they'd made love a million times. As simple as that.

He stopped her. "I don't want you to take care of me."

She looked up, somber. Then she lifted his hands and kissed the backs of his knuckles. His heartbeat thundered. Isabel actually made him dizzy.

"I never did this for anyone else," she said. And finished.

Her attentive touch excited him unbearably. After she'd pulled his shirt out of his trousers, she stepped back. In jeans and a zip-up sweater, she kicked off her shoes and sprawled across the bed.

"Join me," she said. "We can talk. If nothing else happens, it's what was meant."

"You don't understand what you do to me?"

She took on the soft look she had when he kissed her. "Come over here and maybe you'll show me," she said.

He kicked off his shoes, too, and lay down facing her. "We've never shared a bed."

"No." Her wistful smile made that seem like a mistake.

He reached for the zipper on her sweater and pulled it—a little—enough to see more of her breasts than he'd ever seen. Her fullness went to his head. His courage failed. She'd been his best friend's wife.

He put Will out of his head. Isabel slid her hand behind her back, offering herself.

He studied her. "Why aren't you nervous?"

"Look closer." She propelled the zipper a little farther. Her pulse trembled against the pale blue bra he could see straight through. Specks of silver in the material shimmered against her skin with each beat of her heart.

He leaned forward, pressing his tongue to the material that felt surprisingly rough, startlingly sexy. Her deep breath only whet his appetite. He pulled the zipper far enough to bare her. He couldn't wait to take the bra off.

Isabel sat up and pulled her arms out of the sweater, smiling at him with temptation in the curve of her mouth. She rolled onto her back, and he followed, chasing his way with kisses to her nipple. Moisture from his own mouth wet his cheek, as if he'd marked her. He liked her being his.

"Ben," she said, holding his face where she wanted him to kiss. With his hands and his mouth, he stroked her breasts, his excitement rising with hers. Finally, when he couldn't stand waiting one more second, he reached beneath her and undid the catch and then threw the flimsy garment off the bed.

Kissing her bare flesh made him groan with pleasure.

She tasted so good. Spicy and warm and clean and eager for him, her voice catching in short, sharp breaths. She wrapped her legs around his waist in a not-so-subtle plea for more. He lifted his head and found her mouth, pouring his hunger inside her, begging her to need him as much as he craved her. Yearned for her.

Her hands shook as she pushed his shirt off his shoulders. He struggled out of it. They both sighed as he lowered himself, indulging in the thrust of her breasts against his bare chest.

Skin to skin. Too good. Too good to believe.

"I forgot something," she said, her mouth near his ear, making him shudder.

"I didn't, but it's in my coat." He'd remembered protection at the last minute.

"I don't want you to get up." To make moving difficult, she kissed the center of his throat. The tip of her tongue teased him, and she breathed kisses across his chest. Her tongue here, her breath there. *Yes, there again.*

She laughed and he realized he'd spoken out loud.

He laughed, too, but stopped when she circled his nipple with her lips. Selfish in his need, he pulled her against his chest. She didn't seem to mind. As her mouth made him desperate, her hands went to his belt.

"Sit up," she said. She straightened, too, intent on his troublesome buckle, unaware of her bare breasts, pink from his attentions, inviting his hands. He loved the push of her against his palm, but he wanted to see her fingers at his waist.

Her hair fell forward, blocking his view. He pushed it behind her ears, kissing her forehead, but her scent distracted him. He caught her face again, breathing her in as he kissed her.

"I want the smell of you on my skin," he said. "When I dream, your scent is all around me."

With a soft, so-provocative moan, she opened her mouth for his tongue. Somehow they ended up against the pillows, his pants half-off, but she still wore too many clothes. He unbuttoned her jeans, and she unzipped them. He pulled them off, letting his own pants fall. He kicked them away, and went to his coat to take out the condoms.

When he came back to her, she was smiling.

"What?" He dropped the packets beside her and lay across her thighs, pressing a possessive hand to her belly.

"Boxers. I love boxers." She slid her index finger into the waistband, nearly causing him to choke on an indrawn breath.

"Don't do that without warning." He teased her with his own fingertips beneath the brief band of elastic at her hips.

"Don't do this?" She slid her hand farther, tilting

him against her. It wasn't enough, but much stronger pressure and he doubted his own control.

He shifted so he could reach her nipples again, finally licking her breastbone all the way to her navel. Her panties peeled off.

He rose above her and then lay within the cradle of her legs, mimicking the motions of making love to her, easing his own fierce need for a few concentrated moments. Moisture at her temples tasted salty.

"I keep having this urge to thank you," he said between kisses.

"For?"

"How good it feels to lie against you like this, how generous you are."

"Generous? I couldn't have lived much longer without making love to you." She let him see how much she needed him. "You seem to feel the same."

"Oh, yeah." He lingered over her swollen lips. "You're a gift I'm not sure I deserve." He lifted himself and she opened her legs, just enough. He pulled away.

"We'd better…" He didn't finish, but she picked up one of the small packages and opened it.

"Lie back," she said.

He let her put the condom on, but he had to clench his fingers in the bedclothes to keep from wrenching her hands away from him. With a voluptuous sigh, she finally straddled him and lowered herself. Not too much. Teasing him.

He met her, barely hanging on to his slipping control. Isabel closed her eyes and let her fingers drift down his chest, bumping over his nipples till he thought he might explode with strain.

"Look at me," he said.

She obviously tried, but her languid gaze was as potent as her sensual back-and-forth on him. "I know who you are," she said, straight to the point. "I know who I'm with."

"Don't look away." He slid his hands around the curve of her bottom and deepened the stroke that made them both breathe in. Isabel's eyelids drifted again. "Don't," he said.

"I'm self-conscious, Ben. It's too much."

"Uh-huh."

Smiling, she leaned back and trailed her hands up his thighs. "I only want to be with you. No one else will intrude tonight."

"Or ever." He only heard the words after he said them, after he caught the nape of her neck and pulled her close enough to kiss. He lost himself in her taste and took control, pushing her and then pulling back when her cries began to crescendo.

His own body, traitorous with pleasure, nearly betrayed him. He held her still above him, but she still managed to rock—enough to startle them both with her sudden, unexpected release. With a cry, she doubled over and took his mouth.

Silently she demanded he give in. He'd never

realized a woman could match his own passion without trying to hide her feelings as weakness. He submitted—freely.

Her kiss, all woman, all need, dragged him over the edge.

It went on and on. She never closed her eyes. They stared at each other as time and pleasure stretched and slowly, oh so slowly, subsided. At last, when he realized her forearms were shaking beside his shoulders, he pulled her down, onto his chest.

Her heart throbbed against his. Their breathing was a ragged accompaniment to the intimacy they'd created. Intimacy Faith had said he couldn't give her. He didn't want to think about Faith.

"Can we sleep like this for a little while?" Isabel asked, her voice so sexy he wanted her again.

"Mmm-hmm." If he said any more, he might say, "I love you." He felt the words, but he'd just made the best love he'd ever known—with Isabel, of all women.

They both had to be able to trust that words like those didn't just spring from the moment.

RUNNING WATER.

Isabel opened her eyes. The room was dark, but light from the bathroom spilled in an arc that made shadows of a desk and a divan. Ben appeared, naked in the doorway. She frowned. What he needed was light in front of him.

Heat rushed over her at such an indelicate thought. He knelt at the edge of the bed. She lifted her face for the swift touch of his lips.

"You're awake," he said.

"What are you doing?"

"Hoping the house is soundproofed." He looked back. "We'd better not use the jets."

"What time is it?"

"Don't look at the clock."

"Don't look at the clock. Don't close my eyes." She yawned, satisfaction easing every sinew. "You're pretty bossy."

"You're just pretty. No." He pushed her hair off her face and kissed her cheeks, her eyes, her temples. "Beautiful, in every way."

"I like you, too."

"I noticed," he said.

She smiled, hiding her real feelings. She more than liked him. She couldn't imagine ever letting him go back to everyday life alone. She might be falling in love with Ben.

The idea scared her. It could terrify him. They needed more time to be sure.

And they needed to settle the problems that waited outside this room—her parents, his son, her desire to find out if she could live on her own. She pushed those troubles away.

"What do you have in mind?" she asked. With only a smile for an answer, he scooped her out of bcd. She clung to his shoulders. "A hernia for you right now would be most inconvenient for me."

He smiled, as uninhibited as she'd ever seen him. "You can walk on the way back."

But when they reached the tub, he stopped. His face looked different to her, the angles the same, but her feelings for him had changed irrevocably. She'd never see him the old way again.

"Why are you staring at me, Isabel?"

"Just looking. Enjoying."

His smile turned possessive again. She'd come back to Hartsfield, searching for her own way. She wanted no one to own her. But her life felt richer because Ben's expression seemed to say she was his. Terrifying.

"Better put me down," she said.

"I'm afraid I'll drop you if I don't." He let her slide down his body.

"I liked that." She stroked his buttocks. "We could do that again."

"How about a bath first?"

"How handy the faucets are in the middle."

She took one end, sinking into the bliss of bathwater at a perfect temperature, scented with something exotic. "You're going to smell good later," she said.

"I did this for you." His embarrassment made her laugh.

"I know." She laid her arms along the tub, wondering how she'd ever lived before tonight. "It's the ultimate courtship move."

"Ahh." He climbed in at the other end, but he seemed so far away. "I'm glad you approve." He curved his hand around her foot. "What's wrong?"

"You could move closer."

"I like you where you are." With his longer reach, he stroked her thighs.

She sank down as his hands slid higher. Talk ceased. At last, reaching for her waist, he tugged her forward. She went, happy to give him whatever he needed. He pulled her onto his lap, whispering her name in her damp hair.

She had the feeling he was asking her permission.

Again she took over, to show him she wanted to be exactly where she was. The water sloshed gently, teasing her with its own touch as Ben's hands ran restlessly up and down her torso. His clever touch raised her so fast she couldn't wait for him this time.

But she made up for it, reveling in his gruff cries against her throat, in the pressure of his hands as he held her where her body felt best to him.

Finally, they washed and toweled each other dry and staggered back to bed to sleep in each other's arms.

Could rebound love feel this intense? Or could this love be real?

"ISABEL? SORRY, Isabel, but you have to wake up."

She pried an eye open. Nothing romantic about morning. "Go away, Ben."

"I can't." Kneeling again, he lifted a coffee cup from the nightstand. "I went downstairs and begged for caffeine."

"You bring gifts?" She loved his eyes, begging her to wake up. She loved his ruffled hair.

It was damp.

"You've showered. What time is it?"

"Time to move if I'm going to make it home and get Tony to day care."

She sipped the coffee, burned her tongue, swore and set the cup on the table before she crawled out of the bedclothes.

"Are you all right?" Ben asked.

"Laughing wouldn't be your best option." But then she ruined her warning, laughing at herself. She scratched her head and discovered her hair was standing up in spikes. "I'll never look at water the same way."

"You should look at it now." He sipped her coffee, too. "If a cop stops us on the way back, and you look like that, we'll both be taking sobriety tests."

"Suave, Ben." She wished she'd brought a hat. "Do you have a comb?"

"Yes, but shower first and comb in the car."

"You're not trying to get rid of me?"

He stared at her as if she'd lost her mind. Sappy as it might seem, it was a moment she'd treasure forever. He swooped in for a kiss that convinced her of his regret at cutting their time short.

"We'll manage this again," he said. "We just have to be careful."

"You're right. I can't even imagine explaining to Mom and Dad."

After a shower, she found her bag and the clothes she'd packed. Ben had finished her coffee and was dressing hell-bent for leather, too.

"If you don't have time to drive by my house, I could take a cab from yours." She hopped into one pant leg, barely avoiding a tumble to the floor. "Except the sitter would see me."

"I added in time to take you home." He intercepted her curious glance. "Not because I care if the sitter sees you. I don't want to send you home in a cab after last night." He pulled a sweater over his head. "Last night I couldn't believe how confident you were. This morning, I'm the one who's sure."

"Sure we did the right thing?"

"Over and over." His wolfish grin went straight to her heart. There was something sensual in his bad, private joke.

"I'm seeing consequences I ignored last night," she said.

"I promise we'll talk." He took her sweatshirt out of her hands and helped her put it on. With Will, she would have snapped that she wasn't helpless. Ben eased her hair out of her hood, and his touch lingered. He brushed his lips across her forehead. "Let's not forget that comb, though."

They were the first guests out of the B and B, stopping only to thank Cleo. Isabel promised to call later.

Ben drove with awareness Isabel envied. She leaned into her door and nodded off, waking only when he touched her leg or reached for her hand. He walked her to the door at home and kissed her soundly.

"You're all right?" he asked.

"Yeah. Are you okay to drive alone?"

A grin twisted his mouth as he turned. "Your snoring kept me awake, but I think I'll get by."

His tone wrapped her in affection. She'd rather follow him back to his house than do her own tasks today. "I never knew you were a morning person."

"I never knew you weren't." He leaned over the roof of the car. "Come for dinner tonight."

She nodded, hating the moment he drove away. She went inside, climbed her stairs and fell across the bed, praying no one would want to view the house.

Waking later, she showered yet again, restored her hair to a look most humans wouldn't mind and culled her closet for the perfect interview suit.

Ben called at noon. "Getting ready for your appointment?"

"I just found clothes." She closed her mouth, hoping to moisten the dry expanses. "I'm nervous."

"You'll be great. Any organization would have paid event planners a fortune for the work you've done."

"That was good. I needed to hear that, but I'd better go. I'm practicing in the mirror."

"Good," he said, amused.

She didn't remember entertaining Ben so much before. "It's easy for you. You've had the same job since you graduated from college."

"I've been promoted." Just like a man. He had to point out he was climbing the ladder.

"I mean you've proven yourself. I'm worried I'll fall flat on my face."

"You won't. Hold on a sec." He covered his phone to speak to someone else. Then he came back. "I believe in you, Isabel."

"Thanks."

"I'm serious. I'd hire you if it wouldn't be such a conflict of interest. And also, you don't have a chemical engineering degree."

His faith should have comforted her, but it felt too nice to trust. "That's a drawback," she said, trying to control her nerves. "I'm going now."

"Good luck. Bring a change of clothes tonight."

Her pulse banged around her body, but she yanked on the reins. Something had changed for him since last night. She still didn't want to share a bed with him under Faith's roof, and they had to consider Tony, too. "I can't. Tony wouldn't understand."

"You've stayed here—who knows how many times?"

"Never the way you mean." Confused, she tested him. "How would you like to stay here?"

Silence. Thick and unyielding. "I get it. But we'll see you for dinner?"

He and Tony. And her parents.

She'd barely set down the phone when it rang again. "Ben?"

"It's Ray."

"Hi." Ben wouldn't like the arrangements she'd asked Ray to make. She'd almost forgotten. "It's time to ask Ben to join us for a meeting?"

"As soon as possible. Let me check my calendar. You know, I never can work these electronic gadgets. Oh, there it goes. This is Friday—I'm busy till six this evening. How do you feel about Monday?"

"I feel good about it, but Ben won't be enthusiastic."

"He won't turn you down, though."

"I'm not so sure, Ray."

"What you're doing is good for Tony. Ben won't deny his son."

"You must know him better than I do." Her hand trembled. She brought up the other one to help hold the phone. After last night, Ben would feel betrayed that she'd gone ahead with the trust fund without telling him.

A paper rustled on Ray's side of the phone. "He'll be all right once we explain."

"I'll talk to him tonight and then call back for an appointment."

"Okay."

"I'm grateful, Ray. I know all your clients don't get so much of your personal time."

"Happy to help." He coughed with dignity and gruffness, at the same time. "Let me know what Ben says."

"I will." She hung up.

Money didn't matter to Ben. He made plenty for his son. But falling for Ben had only deepened her feelings for the little boy who'd owned her heart since his birth. She wanted him to have the legacy that could give him an easy life.

Ben couldn't see she was only trying to protect her nephew. He feared someone would guess the truth behind Tony's birthright, and his pride stood between him and what was best for Tony—just this once.

CHAPTER TWELVE

"WHAT DO YOU MEAN Ray needs to explain Tony's trust fund?"

The kitchen's flat, shiny surfaces seemed to blind Isabel. Ben's anger vibrated right through her. Without another word, she dragged him out to the deck.

Too late to remember coats. They both gasped in the frigid air.

"Stop, Isabel. You'll freeze out here."

"You were almost shouting." Her mom and dad had taken Tony to play in the living room while Ben and Isabel cleaned up after dinner. Littered with Tony's toys, the house was cozier than Isabel ever remembered it, but the rooms were too open to buffer Ben's raised voice.

She urged him down the stairs, and they crunched through the snow, to the bare bones of Tony's slow-growing tree house. Ben carefully extricated himself from her grasp.

"Tony takes nothing from Will. I told you that."

"I thought you agreed he had the right." She shivered, the damp night and Ben's irate attitude enough to ice her veins.

"If I agreed, I was out of my mind. Why haven't you told me about this?"

"At first, I thought I'd give you time to calm down. Then I got busy and it mostly slipped my mind."

"Mostly."

"All right—I should have told you." Isabel checked the kitchen windows for her parents. "Talk to Ray. Maybe you'll be happier after he explains."

The breeze lifted Ben's hair. His unnatural stillness meant he didn't trust himself to move.

Isabel took a step closer. How far could the wind carry their voices?

"Tony deserves Will's money more than anyone alive, and I can't move on until I deal with the estate. Keep it for school—for an illness. Tony may want it for his own family when he grows up. Let it rot in whatever accounts Ray sets up until Tony decides what he wants to do with it."

Ben flattened one palm across his forehead and then rubbed, as if he were trying to peel off his own skin. "You're forcing me. I don't have a choice."

"It's what you always say. Tony comes first."

The weary lines around his eyes expressed no pleasure and not a lot of resignation. "When do I have to decide?"

"I'm supposed to call Ray today."

"Tonight." He glanced at the black sky. "But I

guess an important client like you has his home number."

She backed away from his sharp tone. "Ben."

"I'm sorry." He came after her, opening his arms.

"Don't." He looked hurt even before she held him off, but no one would ever take that condescending tone with her again. Slipping on an icy tuft of grass, she held up both hands between them. "Even you can't talk to me like that."

"I'm sorry." He slid his hands behind his back as if to reassure her he wouldn't touch her. "But I'd snap Will in two if he was standing in front of me instead of you."

"I'm not Will." She wrapped her arms around her waist. "Even if I seem to have acted like him. And I'm sorry for that."

"I'll talk to Ray." Ben pulled her to him. His mouth against her forehead offered an apology rather than passion. "I'm sorry I took it out on you."

Forgiving Ben came easy. "I know how you feel. Nothing is under our control anymore, and I made it worse. Can you make time on Monday?"

He let her go, as if Monday was too soon. She felt colder, cast out of his warmth.

"They're sympathetic at my office." A question entered his eyes. "I've had things to do for Faith's estate, too, but it was straightforward. She left some jewelry to you, Isabel. I've been wondering how to tell you."

Repulsed, she turned on her heel, beating a path through the frozen grass. "Put it away for Tony's wife."

"Why are you allowed to turn down a bequest?"

"It's different."

"It is different. Will actually fathered my son."

Her heart shattered like icicles hitting the ground. "Ben, I'm not your enemy. I know Tony will never be anyone's child but yours. Will donated sperm and money. You give him love and care and protection. Will visited and played the uncle, but you've been here night and day. You've had more of the good times, but you've also done the dirty work."

He tugged her close again, a man clinging for dear life.

And she tightened her arms.

"Don't let go," he said against her ear.

"What's going to happen to us, Ben?"

"What's wrong?" George asked sharply from the deck.

Isabel edged away from Ben, slowly so they wouldn't look guilty. "Nothing's wrong, Dad."

"We had a small argument." Ben met George halfway across the yard. "Everything's fine now."

"Fine? I heard you from the kitchen."

"Voices carry, Dad." She wished she could bite her tongue off, instead of furthering the story that was starting to smother her. "I have to make a phone call. I'll use the guest room."

She didn't look back.

"WHAT REALLY HAPPENED, Ben? How did you upset my daughter?"

Ben took a deep breath. Lying was easier when he just had to keep his mouth shut. "We were talking about Tony. She thinks he already spends too much time in day care." He'd have to remember to tell her, but it sounded like something she'd say.

"She's always wanted a child of her own. I can see she might get too attached to Tony."

"Too attached?" Before he knew it, he was angry on her behalf—believing his own lie. "Isabel can't be too attached. She's been Tony's second mom since he was born."

"Did he need a second mom?"

"That's an odd question, coming from you. Something on your mind, George?"

"I've noticed how close you and my younger daughter seem to be."

Images of last night tumbled through Ben's mind, and he almost forgot George. "Isabel's important to me."

"And to Tony." George reached for the deck banister and climbed the first step. "She's a responsible woman, and I think she loves Tony as much as you say—as if she were in some way another mother to him. But I wonder if that's healthy for her."

What the hell? "Healthy?"

"How will she make her own life if she feels Tony needs her as much as a mom?"

"He's my son." And he didn't care to think about Isabel making a life that didn't include Tony and him. "But nobody tells Isabel what to do."

"You sound as if you'd like to." George opened the kitchen door. "But you shouldn't take advantage of her soft heart. I want my younger daughter to have what her sister did. A husband who loves her and deserves her—and children of her own."

Ben resisted a slow burn of jealous rage. "I won't stand in her way." Then he remembered he was the husband who'd loved Faith. At last, he felt a first tinge of empathy for his former wife. Neither of them had known the first thing about love in their marriage.

"I'LL HOLD TEN on Monday for you," Ray said. "Call me back if Ben can't make that time."

"Okay. Thanks, Ray."

"I have guests so I must go. I'll check my messages tomorrow if you need to cancel."

He hung up and Isabel did, too, staring at the four sand-colored walls of the guest room she'd used.

Last night's contentment seemed a long way off. She and Ben had slapped a Band-Aid over their problems instead of talking about them. She wasn't a sex-for-sex's-sake kind of woman.

She dropped back, sinking her hands into the

heavy woven comforter. The cloth felt cool against her palms. And real. Not like last night's break in a fairy-tale room, with a man who'd been as desperate for her as she still was for him.

Laughter drifted to her. Tony. His happiness pulled her upright. Why worry about tomorrow or yesterday? She didn't have to solve any more problems this minute. For tonight she'd hang out with Tony and put all complications out of her mind.

Small snags like falling for Ben. She'd loved Will. Surely she'd loved Will. How could she love Ben now? How could she love Ben more? From the gut, from the center of who she was, as deep as the tendons and muscles that held her together.

Another shout of boyish laughter made her turn her head toward the door. She pulled herself together and stood, tired of her own confusion.

Her cell phone rang. She lifted the face and read Leah's number. "Hello?"

"Hi, Isabel. Do you have a moment?"

Leah's mainline Philadelphia manners irritated her more than ever tonight. "Sure. What's up?"

"Well." It was a commentary on Isabel's lack of sophistication. "I'd like to see my son's—grave. Will you come with me?"

Isabel closed her eyes. Last night's sense of safety in Ben's arms flooded back, but he wasn't hers to keep. And last night had been a break from real life and the difficult decisions they both still faced.

"I'd be glad to. When are you coming down?"

"Tuesday? What would you think about that?"

"I'll keep the afternoon free." Maybe she could persuade her mom to come along. The two women had never been best friends, but her mom might remind Leah to be rational.

"I'll call when I'm close to D.C. We can meet at the house."

Not at "your house," but at least not at Will's, either. "Drive carefully."

She hung up and went in search of her mother. Isabel found her mom in the living room, leaning over a small computer on the hearth rug with her Dad and Tony. Behind them, the fire flickered through a wrought-iron screen. Tony chuckled infectiously as he punched the correct button and the small machine played a tune.

"George brought it home today," her mom said. "Tony loves the music."

"Don't we all?" Ben asked wryly.

"It's better than a drum," Isabel said, and he smiled, agreeing.

Tony patted the rug. "Sit, Iz-bell."

He demonstrated a matching game. Every time he clicked on two identical tiles a chime filled the room.

Eventually, Ben groaned from behind the evening newspaper. "I hope we don't lose that thing."

George eased to his feet, muttering as his joints

popped. "It's a grandparent's prerogative to give a child a gift that drives his dad nuts."

Ben shifted his paper aside again. "I'll get my own turn when he grows up?"

Her father actually laughed, more present than he'd been since the day of the funerals. Isabel looked from face to face to face, each warmed by the mellow light of fire and lamp.

"Mom?"

"Hmm?" Her mom was too interested in her grandson's brilliant memory to pay close attention.

"Can I ask you a favor?"

Amelia's surprise startled Isabel. Didn't she ask favors like any normal daughter? "What can I do for you, honey?"

Isabel explained about Leah. "She's more moody than usual right now, and I'm afraid I'll say something ugly if she doesn't lay off. She might not be so—honest—if you're along."

"What time?"

"I'll come, too," Isabel's father said.

"So will I." Ben's protective tone startled Isabel most of all. She avoided looking at him, hoping to keep her parents from noticing.

"We don't all have to go," she said.

"I think it's a good idea." Ben dropped his paper on the floor and went to Tony. "I don't like the way she treats you." He held out his arms for his son. "You— it's time for bed. Let's put your computer away."

"I'll do that," Amelia said. She hugged Tony, who didn't like being parted from his new toy. "Go with your daddy."

"I'll walk you to the stairs." Isabel faked a big yawn. "I have another interview tomorrow."

"Honey," her mother said with regret, "I forgot to ask. How did today's go?"

"Fine." It seemed a long time ago to Isabel. "The office is new and nice. Up-to-date equipment, and they liked me. I'm supposed to go back for a second visit."

"I'm glad to see you taking steps," her father said.

"I had a job in Middleburg, Dad."

"But it didn't feel permanent. This is a choice, not a response to your unfortunate situation."

What had come over him tonight? She didn't miss the telling glance he shared with Ben. "Good night." She kissed both her parents and ran after Tony and Ben.

They were waiting at the bottom of the stairs. Tony kissed her, sharing some cracker crumbs and a whiff of apple juice.

"Night, buddy," she said.

Ben pulled her close. She felt his lips in her hair and pulled away, awkwardly. "I've been trying to get your attention since I called Ray. He asked to see us at ten on Monday."

"Ten." His frown spoke volumes.

"We have to hear what he's arranged."

"For my son."

She jumped, but her parents couldn't have heard his reckless whisper. She took her coat off the banister and put it on, tugging her keys out of the pocket. "I know how you feel. I'd love to shut the door on Barker Synthetics and forget Will ever came near me, but his employees depend on their salaries, and any decisions I make there will affect Tony's future, too."

"At least you played some role in the company."

"You're wrong. Will made sure I didn't." She opened the door. "I thought some wrongheaded sense of being a provider made him shut me out, but now I wonder what else he was hiding."

"Don't drive yourself crazy. Even I don't think he had time for any more games." He pointed at her car. "Start the engine. Let it warm up."

"I will, but you all go on upstairs. You must be cold."

Again he lowered his voice. "I wish you'd stay and warm me like last night."

"Maybe last night was a mistake, too."

His tone roughened. "Now, who's looking for excuses?"

"I am."

"Because I got too close to you." In an instant he became her lover again, his feelings naked on his drawn face.

"Yes," she said. "Too soon." Panic filled her at

the thought of committing to a man, especially the one who had an ax to grind with anyone named Barker.

"We've both been alone inside broken marriages for too long." Ben glanced at the living room doorway. "I'm ready for you, Isabel, and I'm not turning back. I won't let you turn back, either."

His confidence frightened her. She headed into the frigid darkness.

"HE WANTED to talk about our relationship in the middle of the hall." With a glance at her watch, Isabel turned from the forever-view outside Ray's floor-to-ceiling windows. "With my parents in the next room, and my mom asking me questions all the time. And my dad's obviously said something to Ben that I don't know about."

"What relationship?"

Ray's shock made her realize what she'd admitted. If she and Ben worked out their problems, everyone they knew would be stunned to find them together.

"Ben and I have been seeing each other." Did that sound insensitive? Ray ducked behind his usual expression of lawyerly indifference. "We didn't mean for anything to change between us after Will and Faith died."

Ray stared. She floundered in silence.

"What changed?" he asked.

"Everything."

"My God. Your parents will never understand. I wouldn't."

Isabel rubbed her chest. Her sweater seemed to be choking her. Even Ray, who knew everything, thought she and Ben were wrong together.

The door opened. "Mr. Jordan," Pam said. She broke off to stare at Ray's disturbed expression. Fortunately, she was too professional to ask what was going on.

Isabel stood as Ben walked in. His eyes searched her face. He took the chair next to hers.

"Hello, Ray."

"Ben." Ray looked a bit like a father who'd forgotten exactly where he'd left his shotgun. He began to restack the legal documents in front of him. "Shall we start?"

"I'd be grateful. I have to pick up Tony from day care in two hours, and I'd like to beat the traffic." Ben shrugged. "I know Isabel told you the truth."

"That's right." And Ray started going over the trust fund. Ben stiffened when the other man turned the first page toward him. Isabel saw the amounts through his eyes and braced herself in case he threw the stack of documents at her.

He took a deep breath that pushed him back in the chair. He spun the page toward Ray. "I can't take this." He turned to Isabel. "Not even from you."

"You have no choice, and I need to finish with

this." She begged with her eyes and her hand on his arm.

Ray continued with the trust fund. "You're in charge, Ben. Once we sign these papers, I'll set up the appropriate accounts. I'd like to suggest an investment counselor for you. With these funds as a start, Tony will never have to worry about money."

"Why isn't Isabel in charge?"

"I don't want to be." She hoped they weren't about to start this argument again. "You're Tony's dad. You know what he needs. This money belongs to him."

"I've described everything as a gift from his uncle. You'll decide what to tell him as he matures."

"How can this be right?" Ben stood. "I didn't earn it."

"Will would want Tony to have it." Ray leaned forward. "I knew Will all his life. I wouldn't have believed he could hurt Isabel or you." He shook his head and turned back to the papers. "The Will I knew took responsibility for his employees and his wife and I believe he'd have wanted this for your son."

"I see the point in everything you and Isabel are saying, but Will was my best friend and he all but ruined my life. How can I take money from him that I never could have made for my boy?"

"Because it belongs to Tony," Ray said. "It will make his life easier."

"And a real man wouldn't let his pride get in the

way of doing what's best for his son." Ben reached for the pen Ray was holding out to him. "I'd like the name of the investment counselor. I'll feel best if I don't have to touch this fund."

"I understand."

Ben tried to smile but ended up looking bleak. "Thank you, Isabel. Are you sure you trust me with a sum like this?"

She wished she could put her arms around him. Ray's presence stopped her. "I'm pretty sure Tony can trust you."

Ray pushed a sheet across the desk. "Sign where I've marked, Ben. I'll put together a package for you, including the investment firm's name. But call if you have any questions."

Ben signed and then set down the pen. "Thanks," he said. "I appreciate your help."

Embarrassment lowered his voice as he adjusted to compromise. Not caring what Ray thought, Isabel ran her hand down Ben's back. His muscles tightened beneath her palm.

He'd accepted the gift to Tony with better grace than she might have managed in his place.

CHAPTER THIRTEEN

THE NEXT DAY, Ben left work early and headed to The Children's Cottage. He wanted to get Tony back home to the sitter before Leah arrived at Isabel's place.

As he drove, he noticed the sheaf of papers he'd left on the passenger seat the night before. The astounding total in Tony's trust fund swam before Ben's eyes. How he'd managed to speak to Isabel and Ray at all, he'd never be able to say.

Urged on by the tatters of dignity Faith and Will's affair had left him, he'd wanted to walk out of Ray's office.

He'd been so busy resenting Will he hadn't realized he'd hated the fact that Isabel could do more for his son than he could.

At The Children's Cottage, he picked up Tony, who refused to be carried to the car. His efforts at skipping left him swinging on Ben's arm.

"'Kip, Dad!"

"Excellent skipping, Son."

"Uh-uh." Tony pulled back on Ben's hand. "You 'kip."

"In front of…" He didn't finish. What better way to learn humility? Without looking at the windows behind them, he and Tony skipped beneath a cloudy sky, along the sidewalk to their car. It took a while, but they made it and his son patted his shoulder in approval as he fastened the car seat.

"Thanks, buddy." Ben ducked his head for a quick kiss. Tony smelled of sweat from playing hard, milk from lunch and a faint hint of plastic from his SpongeBob mat. All comfortingly familiar.

"Less go!" Tony pointed with his index finger, and Ben's smile grew tight. Faith had taught Tony that gesture. He hadn't done it since she'd died.

"Let's go," Ben agreed. He took his spot behind the steering wheel, smiling at Tony in the rearview mirror. His son would be better off if Ben learned to live in peace with Faith's memory.

The sitter was already waiting. George and Amelia had left a message with her that they'd meet him at Isabel's. Leah had also arrived by the time Ben joined them.

Isabel looked harried when she opened the door. "Hey," she said, and then stood close. "Thank God. I was afraid you wouldn't make it."

"Is she in a bad mood?"

Isabel pulled him inside, clinging to his hand. "She's tense so she's offered decorating tips and she cleaned my kitchen counter, all the while noting her son was accustomed to a tidier housekeeper."

Ben checked that the coast was clear and kissed her swiftly. "Maybe that was what he saw in Faith."

Isabel's color rose. "My counter was clean."

"I was trying to make a joke."

"Oh." She turned toward the kitchen but then stopped. "You joked about Faith."

"I know." He kissed her again for noticing. "It must be growth."

Leah came around the counter in question as he entered the kitchen. "You're here at last. Can we go, Isabel?"

Nodding, Isabel plucked two cellophane-wrapped bouquets from the fridge.

"I'd be glad to drive." Ben would prefer Isabel didn't have to fend off her mother-in-law's nasty remarks, drive and face Will's grave again all at once.

"Will your vehicle fit all of us?" Leah asked.

Faith had insisted on the largest SUV available at the time Tony had been born. "Easily," he said.

They piled in, Leah taking the front seat as her due. Maybe she suffered from motion sickness. One more jab at Isabel, and he'd welcome the opportunity to suggest she ride in the back with her head out the window for fresh air.

"Leah, you weren't well enough to attend Will's funeral?" George asked from the second seat.

"That, and Isabel didn't leave me enough time to prepare. She insisted he be buried right away."

In the third seat, Isabel leaned her head back and

closed her eyes. Ben happened to know she'd offered to send a car for Leah when she couldn't get to Philadelphia in time to pick up her mother-in-law and drive back herself.

He entered the cemetery through black arching iron gates and rolled down the narrow roads to Will's grave. His annoyance faded a little when he noticed Leah twisting her hands so hard she must be hurting herself. As soon as he parked, Isabel climbed out and came around to assist her former mother-in-law.

"This won't be easy," she said.

"Which is why we've all come." Amelia joined them on Leah's other side. "On a day like today, you all need moral support. And we loved Will, too."

Isabel climbed the small hill first. She laid her bouquet on the mound of raw earth. Ben hardly recognized her drawn, sad yet angry expression. She handed the other bouquet to Leah, who laid it beside Isabel's and then patted the flowers, taking unconscious comfort in stroking the clear wrap.

Tears streaked the older woman's makeup, but she wasn't through with Isabel. "Look at all these dead arrangements. Why haven't you come by to clean these out?"

The vitriol in her tone was unexpected. "I didn't think," Isabel said with a desperate look, but Ben's protective instincts had already brought him to her side. She'd said Leah reacted to grief with anger, but Leah had chosen the wrong target.

Amelia quickly took a spot across from them. "I don't think you understand everything my daughter's had to face, Leah."

And she didn't know the half of it. He slid his arm around Isabel's waist and she leaned into him. Leah noticed.

"You're still friends, then."

Neither he nor Isabel answered. He didn't trust himself. It was as if everything, Faith and Will's betrayal, his fear of losing Tony, his imperative to keep Isabel safe from any more harm, all coalesced into rage that was focused on Leah and her irrational attacks.

Their silence just appeared to egg her on. "What did you do to him, Isabel? Why did you force my son to throw you out of his home?"

"He didn't." Pain made her sharp. "What's the matter with you?"

"If you'd been home, he wouldn't have been driving your sister cross-country in a snowstorm. He always said it was easier to travel than face that house and you."

"Cut it out, Leah," Ben broke in to her accusations. "Isabel's not your punching bag."

But Isabel gasped. "Is that true?"

"Hell, no," Ben said, trying to turn Isabel to face him, but she obviously thought Leah might know Will's secrets.

"I'd lie? Now, when I'm seeing the truth of my son's sad life? He was lonely because you weren't a good wife to him. He died, helping a friend. Why couldn't you drive your own wife, Ben?"

Isabel wrapped her fingers around his wrist. "Don't," she said, as he moved forward. "She's realizing how long forever is. She'll never see him again."

"Don't patronize me, young woman. I should have spoken to you about making my son happy, because he told me you'd said you didn't want to be his wife. You didn't want to be any man's wife."

Both George and Amelia turned considering looks on Isabel. She'd explained nothing about the breakup, trying to protect Faith's reputation—trying to protect Ben, too.

"Why didn't you give my son his freedom earlier? Why did you have to waste the last years of his life?"

"*Enough,*" Ben said. "Your son was preparing you for the story he gave me—that Isabel had cheated on him. But he was lying to cover his own adultery. He had a mistress for at least three years. He took those trips so he could travel with her. *He* abandoned Isabel. He's the one who turned his back on their marriage. He even had a son with her."

Ben stopped breathing. What had he done?

Amelia suddenly gasped. "He traveled with… that's why they had the bags."

"No, Mom." Isabel tried to stop her.

"It was Faith." She turned to Isabel. "This wasn't the first trip they took together. I remember—about six months ago, you called and asked to speak to Faith, but she wasn't with us. You said you must have misunderstood her plans, and I thought she must have lied to you for a good reason, so I covered for her. I didn't know where she was, but I told you she'd gone out to dinner with a friend."

"My God," Isabel said, stark fear in her eyes.

Ben couldn't speak at all, but he was grateful for her arms, suddenly tight around his waist.

"My son had a bastard child?" Unaware she'd finally lit the fuse of his rage, Leah sounded as if she'd discovered Will was a serial killer. Ben was already halfway to her when Isabel yanked him back.

"Leah, he's your grandson," she said. "Don't ever call him that again."

"I can't have that. Do you know how old my family name is?"

Ben's only thought was to shut her mouth. He'd caused this.

"Or how many socially correct bastards you've paraded around Philadelphia?" Isabel clung to Ben's coat. She turned to him. "Don't worry. She can't hurt us."

"Tony isn't yours?" Amelia finally caught on, but her eyes shone. Her smile, wide and trembling, betrayed terrible happiness. He wanted to be sick.

Fear, as cold as the ice in his collar, urged him to run to his car and drive to his son.

"Why did you—?" Isabel asked, but her fear became compassion. She stood in front of him. "Mother, stop before you ruin what's left of our family."

Stop before I take my son to parts unknown. How had his temper spiraled so out of control? He'd begged Isabel not to tell, and he'd managed to spew most of the truth, his only thought to defend her.

"Tony belongs with us."

"No, Mother."

"No," Ben said, moving Isabel out of his way. "Stop and think."

Amelia scowled at Leah. "That woman won't want the embarrassment of him. Ben's not his biological father. We have the right to keep him."

"My son would never do such a thing. Sleep with his wife's sister?" Leah hadn't yet caught up.

"Amelia," George said, "why would you think of taking Tony from Ben?"

"He's our flesh and blood." She grabbed his arm. "He's ours, George. It's like having a second chance with Faith."

"Tony's going nowhere." Ben reached into his pocket for his keys. "He's mine and he stays with me."

"Mom, please," Isabel said again, and he stared at her. She shouldn't be begging. She should be as angry as he was.

"There's no question." He pulled away from her. "I'm going home to my child."

"My grandson," Amelia said.

"You're out of your mind. I'm the only father he's known." He sounded certain, even to himself, except for the tears that made his voice tremble. "No court in the land would take him from me."

"No court would deny him to his only blood relatives." Amelia reached for Isabel, who struggled away from her mother but didn't take his side, either. "Why didn't you tell us?"

"Because I love Tony, and I won't do anything to hurt him. He's lost his mother. Have you heard him cry for her in his sleep? Do you want to make him cry for Ben?"

She glanced at Leah, who actually sat, dumbfounded, on a nearby tombstone. "I didn't know Will at all."

"Neither did I." Isabel looked from her mother to Ben. "But I know Tony is going to suffer if you don't talk this out. Do the right thing for him."

"Talk?" Disgusted, Ben looked for his car. With his heart breaking, he couldn't seem to remember where he'd left it. All he could think of was Tony crying, for Faith, for Isabel, even for Will. Thanks to his own foolish temper, his son could be crying for him tonight. He wouldn't even know why his father had disappeared. Amelia, in her elated mood, could easily drag his boy to Pennsylvania before nightfall.

"Don't walk away, Ben. You have to talk to my parents."

Apparently, Isabel thought blood mattered most, too. "There's nothing to say. Tony stays with me." He started down the hill. "You'd better call a cab for your family. They aren't welcome in my house anymore."

"Ben, wait."

He turned. She hadn't moved. She was still standing at her mother's side, while her father, shell-shocked, stared from one of them to the other.

"Come with me," he said, his tone still cracking. He'd been so close. Isabel had begun to fall in love with him. They could have made a family for his baby.

God, never to touch Tony's hair again or hold his hand as he crossed a street. Never to read about trains or sing that music-class song he loved so much.

"Isabel?" He wouldn't beg. Not again. Had she been the one using him? To make sure he didn't run away with Tony?

"Don't ask me to choose," she said.

"You've made your choice," Ben said. "I don't have one, and neither does Tony. My son has one parent left, and I won't give him up while I'm alive."

And all this had happened because he'd tried to protect the woman he'd thought he could love. Love never had done much for him.

ISABEL HELPED Leah into her car while her parents went inside the house.

"You think I'm a monster, don't you?" Leah asked.

"Right now, yes."

"I brought all this on myself. I went too far, but I was so hurt. I suddenly realized my son was gone forever."

"I know." Isabel blamed her mother-in-law, too, but she was more interested in talking her own mother out of her self-seeking plan.

"I get angry and then I say things I don't even mean—because I want someone else to hurt."

That made Isabel focus. "Leah, you've hurt me more than you could have wanted to. I know you're mad I'm alive and Will's dead, but you've destroyed a father and son."

"It was Ben who said enough to clue your mother in."

"You did this. You goaded Ben by trying to hurt me."

"Maybe so, maybe so." Real tears flowed down Leah's cheeks, but Isabel hardly cared. "He could have kept quiet."

"He may have lost his son. Would you have liked watching someone else bring Will up? Knowing you could never claim him again?"

"I don't know what to say."

"Tell me you won't be back." Isabel straightened. "If you take one step in Tony's direction, I'll call every major newspaper in Pennsylvania, and they'll hear exactly what happened today. The Barker family would be human interest. Especially, the matriarch calling her grandson a filthy name."

Leah finally had the grace to look ashamed. "You do think I'm a monster. I ache for my son, but I'm sixty-two years old. I don't have the energy to raise a little boy now. I hope you sort this out so that I get to see him occasionally, but I know my limits."

"Well, you hurry home and I'll try to clean up the mess." Isabel had tried all her married life to treat Leah with respect and compassion. For the first time, she fought back. But she should have made that a habit before this afternoon.

She was in her own house before Leah got out of the driveway. True to form, her mother had busied herself making coffee. When she was upset or sad or too happy to believe her own supposed good luck, she had to work off her energy.

"Mother."

"I don't understand you, Isabel."

"Dad, talk some sense into her."

"I wonder if she's right, honey. Ben tried to hide the truth."

"With me telling him he should trust you the whole time." She felt sick. "Don't 'honey' me. Tony knows one father, one home. I won't help you take him away from Ben."

"You're on his side?"

Her mother sounded hurt. Isabel didn't want

to hurt anyone. "I'm on Tony's side, Mom. Faith wouldn't want you to do this."

"Yes, she would."

"She was taking him away when she died," Isabel's father said. Her mother all but clapped her hands, in her rush to agree.

"And she was wrong. You'd know she was wrong if you could look beyond what you want."

"Ben can visit."

"Visit?" Isabel made no attempt to hide her shock. "Visit his own son?"

"Why are you so sure he's right?" her dad asked.

"Because he's Tony's dad. No one can take Ben's place with him."

"No, there's more," Amelia said. "George, think back to the cemetery."

"Are you two ganging up on me?"

"I'm trying to make sense of the fact that you've obviously known that little boy is not Ben's child but you didn't tell us." She looked at her husband. "Why did Ben lose his temper? Does a man risk so much for a friend?"

"What are you saying?" George turned faintly green. "You and your sister fell in love with each other's husbands?"

"No." Not exactly true, but she put a lot of power into that "no." She imagined Ben, holding his son, believing he had finite time with Tony. His anguish was hers, and she didn't care any more what her parents thought. "I'm in love with Ben now, but I saw him only as Faith's husband and Will's friend—my best friend—before I came back here."

"I hate to sound like Leah," her mother began.

"Then you'd better not. I'm running short on forgiveness, and I don't see how you can turn on Ben and Tony because you want a little bit of Faith back."

"You've never lost a child. I carried her for nine months inside my body. She was supposed to outlive me, have grandchildren of her own."

"And be faithful to her husband," Isabel said. "She left him a note to tell him about Tony. Like you, she thought donating sperm and the occasional visit was fatherhood."

"Don't talk to your mother like this," her dad said.

"Mom, put Tony ahead of your grief."

Her mother shook her head, ignoring her grandson's pain to nurse her own. "You think you can marry that man and have all the time you want with Tony." Her expression changed. Realization dawned on her pale face. She slammed the coffee carafe on the counter so hard it shattered. "That man took advantage of you so he'd have a better shot at keeping our grandson."

"I'm leaving."

Neither her mother nor her father tried to stop her. Isabel found her keys. Despite still-snowy roads, she drove as fast as she could to Ben's house, half expecting to find it empty and him on the way to Canada.

He opened the door with Tony on his elbow and a wary look on his face. "Are you here to stay?" he asked.

"You mean am I taking your side against my parents?"

He nodded.

"Not exactly."

He walked away.

Over his shoulder, Tony held out his arms, his face puckering with tears. She shut the door and followed them. "I tried talking to Mom and Dad. Why did you say anything? Leah was working off steam."

"Someone needed to pry her off your back years ago." In the kitchen, he put Tony in his high chair.

"But what do you always say? Tony comes first."

Ben straightened and looked at her. If she trusted her instincts at all, she'd swear love looked at her from his eyes. "I guess you matter to me as much as Tony does," he said.

Her legs wobbled. She reached for the wall to keep from falling down. "You matter that much to me, too."

"And you'll stand by me in court?"

"Oh." She braced against the wall with both hands. Could her mother have been right? Had he been using her? "You think a judge will choose you if I'm with you."

"You're Tony's aunt."

"That's what the other night was about. That's

why you asked me to stay here and why you said I mattered. I've been your backup plan." How could she talk so reasonably when she wanted to scream and cry and swear she'd learn not to love him?

"What?" he asked.

"You're good. You look shocked." She pushed off the wall. "I don't know why my mother and father are willing to be so cruel, but I won't side against my family." She stopped at the kitchen door. "About the night we spent together?"

He hadn't moved. He didn't speak. She relished the dread in his eyes. He knew pain was about to come.

"You put on a hell of a show," she said. "I hate that you wasted so much time on me, but Will had nothing on your act."

CHAPTER FOURTEEN

ISABEL SOLD the house at the end of February. On Valentine's Day, she'd started working at Linder and Farnes Advertising as a copywriter. Writing with admiration for toilet paper and insurance and frozen crab didn't come easy when she felt numb as an iceberg.

Almost every day, her parents' attorney called. She refused to speak to him, but she kept trying to convince her mother and father they were being selfish, rather than showing love for Tony.

Ben's attorney called three times. She didn't talk to him, either. Ben called often the first several days after their last argument, but she had nothing to say. He'd made her believe in him and his feelings—lies that had become as important as life's blood to her.

He finally left a message while she was at work one day, to say that she could visit Tony. She called him back and, over the phone, they agreed she'd pick up Tony at day care.

"You won't take him to your mom and dad?" Ben asked.

"How can you ask? I kept the secret. They're hardly speaking to me anyway."

"I want to talk to you."

"No, Ben. I'll drop Tony off after dinner and some time at the park."

"Will you stay for a few minutes?"

"No."

She was too vulnerable. Even knowing he'd used her, she didn't trust herself. She wanted him—damn her soul—she loved him too much.

"I meant everything we said and did that night," Ben told her in a ragged voice. "I love you. I just need for you to choose me and Tony. Is that so much to ask?"

"You want me to turn my back on my parents and prove that you matter most. I'm not Faith's second string," she said, harking back to his statement about Will the night they'd first kissed.

She spent a poignant afternoon with her nephew. He'd learned to say Grandma and Grandpa sometime during their visit. Hearing him ask for them broke her heart. She returned him to Ben, whose sad eyes almost drew her inside. She didn't set foot in his house.

When the subpoena came, she called Ray.

"Your parents subpoenaed you?" He couldn't believe it, either.

"I won't say they're best for Tony."

"Do you still think Ben is?"

"Yes, but if I say that, I'm not sure Mom and Dad will ever forgive me."

"I assume you told them you thought Tony should be with Ben?"

"Because it's true."

"I don't know why they'd call you, unless they think you'll take the stand, look at them and collapse in their favor."

"Even if I'm looking at them, I'll be seeing Tony."

"I'll go to court with you if you want me to, but you don't need me. My best advice is to do what you can for your nephew."

"I wouldn't mind having a friend, Ray."

"Give me the date."

"Thanks. I can never pay you back."

"You may get a bill, though. Call your mother and father one more time."

She did, to no avail. Her mother kept insisting Faith would want her to raise Tony.

Isabel never tried to talk Ben out of fighting. It was the closest she came to choosing him over her parents.

THE WORST HAPPENED. Her day to testify came. She'd hoped that her mother and father would walk in, take one look at the courtroom and come to their senses. No such luck.

She, on the other hand, began to cry as she looked out from the witness stand. On one side her mother sat with a plea in her eyes, her father embarrassed but hopeful next to her. At least he had some idea they were in the wrong. On the other side, Ben was gaunt, as haunted as a man who'd already lost his only child.

The bailiff swore her in. Her parents' attorney, Mr. Loggins, stood.

"Mrs. Barker, how long have you known the child was no biological relation to Mr. Jordan?"

Isabel turned to her mother, silently begging her to stop the questioning. Her mom looked away.

"Since three months before my husband died," Isabel said. "About seven months now."

"And you never told your parents?"

She crossed her arms. "Was it their business?"

"Your Honor," Mr. Loggins said.

"Answer, please." The woman behind the bench, starched and tidy in her black robe and matching hair, remained the picture of objectivity.

"I didn't tell them."

"Because you knew they had rights to raise their grandchild, and Mr. Jordan has no rights at all to this innocent boy who's lost his mother and true father?"

Isabel looked immediately at Ben. Before, he would have lost his temper. Today, he looked as if someone had knifed him. They'd danced around Will's role in Tony's life so many times, hardly ever admitting it out loud. It hurt too much to bear. "When

I learned the truth, my sister and my husband were still alive. They chose not to tell my parents."

"Mrs. Barker, answer my question. You knew they had the right to raise their grandson."

"That wasn't my reason for keeping silent," she said. Again, she implored her mother to end this mistake.

"Why did you hide the truth your parents deserved to hear, Mrs. Barker?"

"Objection, Your Honor," Ben's attorney said. "Does Mr. Loggins intend to continue testifying for this witness?"

"A little less hyperbole, Mr. Loggins," Judge Simkins said. "Please answer the question, Mrs. Barker. I'd like to hear your opinion."

She tried to say out loud in the courtroom that Tony's only place was with Ben. With her mother and father watching her as if she held the key to their dreams of a second chance with Faith, she couldn't do it.

"Mom, please help me." She spared a swift glance at Ben. "I'm torn between you, and I love you all. I don't want to hurt any of you."

"Just say what you believe, honey."

Ben's lawyer stood again. The judge waved him down. "This is family court. I'm for a little leeway if the parties can talk to each other."

Isabel shot her a look of thanks. "We can make a family for Tony, without court dates and custody and visitation schedules. He loves his father. He won't understand why you want to take him away from Ben." She wiped her eyes. "Can't you see how much Tony's lost already, and now you're going to make sure he has no dad? You're not that selfish, Mom."

"Mrs. Barker, do you need a moment?" Mr. Loggins asked.

"I need a miracle. Someone with clear eyes who loves my nephew." She stared from her mother to her father. "Tony trusts us. You're putting him in the same position I'm in right now. One day he'll look at you and Dad and know if he chooses Ben, he breaks your heart. Then he'll look at Ben and know that if he chooses you, Ben may not forgive him. Tony's not going to forget his father. He may even think Ben abandoned him, that he did something to make Ben stop loving him."

"Stop." From the respondent's table, Ben stood. "You don't have to do this."

Now that she'd started, she refused to give in. "You have to keep fighting. Sit down before you get in trouble."

"You do love him more than us," her father said.

The gallery rustled.

"Mom, how are you going to drag Tony out of that house screaming for Ben? Ben is his daddy. He couldn't care less about blood or genetics. When he gets ready for bed at night, he wants Ben's arms around him. He wants Ben singing him to sleep."

"Your Honor," Loggins said again, "shouldn't we have a little order?"

"No." Amelia took over, and Isabel felt relief at the realization in her eyes. "We should show real love for my grandson." She covered her cheeks as she tried to explain what she'd done. "I do want him. I've lost my daughter, my baby girl, who loved her son and loved me. I just wanted to see her in Tony. Every day—in my house—sleeping in her bed—going to her school. I needed something of Faith back."

"But she's gone, Mom, and we have to love Tony generously." Isabel wasn't sure Faith would have remembered how much Tony needed the only father he'd ever known, but she chose to believe her mother could see the best way for Tony. "He comes first, as he would have with Faith."

Ben's hand hit the table with a thud. Tears stood in his eyes. He stared at Amelia with intensity that should have set the room on fire.

Amelia put her head down. "I'm sorry, Ben. I lied to myself because I felt as if God had given me an other chance with my daughter when I found out the truth. But I used to sing to her when she went to bed. Maybe that's why she started singing to Tony. No one would have had any right to take my place with my daughter. Your place is with him."

"I'd give up my life for Tony." Ben licked his lips. "I'll even let you and George be his grandparents again. Tony needs us all."

"Mr. Loggins, what do we do to give my son-in-law custody?" She slid her hand through the papers on the table.

"Your Honor, I'm not sure my client understands she's throwing away her case." Loggins scrambled for his notes, clearly unused to this kind of resolution.

"I think your client is learning to love her grandchild. We like families to stay together, and these people may have talked themselves into a second chance to give Tony all the love he deserves." She banged her gavel. "You're excused, Mrs. Barker."

BEN DROVE and didn't let himself think until he reached Isabel's house. It looked as silent as it had every other day in the week since he'd been given custody of his son. She might be out again.

He had to knock. He couldn't leave without making sure.

He'd barely lifted his hand when she opened the door. "Where's Tony?" she asked.

Just looking at her made him feel whole. He wanted to take her soft hair between his fingers, breathe in her scent that was life to him. He needed to hold her. "I left him with a sitter. This is about you and me."

She didn't throw him out. She didn't ask him in, either. But when she walked away, she left the door open. Close enough to an invitation.

"I'm sorry," he said, painfully aware of the new packing boxes in the hall.

"You won. Why should you be sorry?"

"I lost you." She put the table with its empty rose bowl between them. "I got scared when your parents found out. I thought I needed you to prove I came first."

"I never told my mom and dad."

"Who knew I'd take care of that?"

"You should have wanted me no matter whose side I took."

"Could you live with a woman who helped her parents take your child?"

She looked down, shaking her head. "I admit it was an impossible situation." A faint smile lifted her mouth, and hope showed itself. "Did you say—live with a woman?"

"Maybe you should ask your mother how I really feel. She's a cross between Sherlock Holmes and Suzy Homemaker."

"She wouldn't like that Suzy Homemaker part."

"Are we still friends, Isabel?"

"I don't want to be your friend anymore."

His hope died a painful death. He rubbed his chest, trying to reach the broken pieces. "I love you, not because of Tony or because I'm out for revenge against Will and Faith. I love you. I'm home where you are. I'm in a rush to make love to you because I can't believe you want me as much as I want you. I want my son to grow up at your knee, and I hope we'll make more babies, brothers and sisters for

Tony. When I look at you, I see the future. I trust the future." His voice broke again and again. He didn't care. She already knew what kind of man he was. "My future and Tony's is with you. Trust us with yours, and believe I'll never again ask you to make a choice that hurts."

"Ben, I love you. I'll choose you all my life," Isabel said through tears he cherished. "I went to Pennsylvania to make sure Mom and Dad were all right. I would have come to you."

"Then come home now." He realized what he'd said. "Later, we'll sell the house and start over in one that's only ours."

She put her arms around his waist. "I don't want to make Tony move."

Ben held her, wondering how he could ever let her go. "Since we're making your home, too, we'll find a new place for us all."

"Thanks for offering." She lifted her face and he had to kiss her. Her eyes sang. He took her mouth with the love of a real husband. When he raised his head, she looked as dazed as he felt. "But maybe," she said, "we just clutter your house a little and make it our own."

He tipped her chin to kiss her throat. He couldn't taste enough of her. "I can't believe you're mine."

"Easiest choice I ever made," she said.

"Can we go upstairs? I'd like to make love to you before we go home to Tony."

She glanced upward.

He read her thoughts again. "Will's not here anymore."

"I thought you might have forgotten this was his house, too."

"I don't care. Will has nothing to do with us. I love you."

"You'd better come show me."

They spent the afternoon in her guest room, proving all they'd ever need to know to each other. Finally, exhausted, they slept. As night began to creep into the room, Ben woke in his lover's arms.

"Will you marry me, Isabel?"

"So soon? Don't you want to be sure?"

"Do you still need to live on your own?"

"If I did?" she asked.

"I'd better admit I can see this is a test. I'll wait if you ask me, but I'm only going to be more sure every moment we're together."

"We'll argue sometimes."

"You can't talk me out of marriage." He ran his hand down her back to curve it over her bottom. "No one loves like you do without forever on her mind."

Laughing, Isabel slid out of bed and disappeared into the bathroom. She hadn't answered his proposal.

"I'm taking a shower," she said over the running water.

He'd never been in the bathroom up here. He

flipped the light switch as he went inside. "It's perfect, a box made for two."

"Turn off the light." She opened the shower door and sprawled on the marble bench inside.

"No." He followed her in and pulled her onto his lap. "I want to see you."

ALMOST TOO WEAK to walk, Isabel dressed while Ben called home. She ran downstairs and pulled a package out of the sideboard. It was for Tony.

Ben came down the stairs, shutting his phone. "The sitter already fed him. It's later than I thought."

"We took a long shower." Isabel's heart beat a rapid tattoo as she remembered his skin sliding against hers, his need growing inside her. Her own cry, which always seemed to drive him over the edge. "We should try out yours later."

"Will you stay tonight?"

"Let me pack a bag." Upstairs, she packed her gift for Tony as well as work clothes and a nightgown she didn't intend to wear.

Ben had already started the car when she came back down. "I didn't want you to be cold," he said against her mouth.

"No more seduction." She slid her hand through his hair. This man belonged to her. "I'm dying to see Tony."

Reluctantly she moved away from him and they

locked up. At Ben's house, the sitter called a hello from the kitchen. Isabel waited while he paid her. Then they found Tony in the living room, holding the fireplace poker and broom.

Ben rushed to take them from his son's hand. "Hey, Tony, no drumming with those."

"Dad." It was more "come on" than greeting.

"No," Ben said again.

"I missed seeing you together."

Tony finally saw her. "My Iz-bell!"

She clutched him in a hug that felt desperate. She'd almost lost him and his father. Her family. She kissed his forehead with a loud smack.

"Look what I have." She opened her bag and pulled out a SpongeBob coloring book and crayons. "Just for you, buddy."

Clapping, Tony dropped his brand-new box of crayons and then bent to grab them. Isabel opened the box. Ben opened the coloring book. Over Tony's head, they shared a look of love that felt right—it felt steadfast. "Jellyfishing, Tony?" he asked.

Tony seemed to be explaining how it was done. Isabel moved to an ottoman beside Ben. While he listened to Tony, she kissed the top of her lover's head and pushed her hand down his broad chest.

"Iz-bell, color." Tony offered her a blue crayon.

She took it and then slid to the floor at Ben's feet. "I wonder if he's jealous?"

"He'll get used to us, too."

"Are you hungry?" Isabel colored where Tony pointed, a big shell on the edge of the page.

"I'll make something for us." He lifted her hair off her nape. "Do you really think you can feel at home in this house?"

"We're about to find out." She turned his hand and kissed his palm, loving the way his eyelids immediately drooped. "We start a new life tonight. Here."

EPILOGUE

Six months later

STOPPING IN FRONT of the small blue Cape Cod, Ben parked at Amelia and George's curb. Isabel resisted a now-familiar tension.

Even after six months of seeing her and Ben together, her parents still tried to look through them. The court case had left wounds. On top of that, they didn't seem to understand Ben was her true love.

"It's all right." His hand on her thigh had grown oh-so-sweetly familiar. "Tony will win them over eventually because we've made him happy."

He looked content, drooling in his sleep.

"I don't know how you stand this, Ben."

"I love you and Tony, and I still care about George and Amelia. They're important to my family."

Isabel leaned across the console, taking strength in his nearness. His life and hers were linked in ways that continued to surprise her. She thought of him first when something happened at work. She thought of him when something odd happened on the metro. She just naturally thought of Ben first.

"Gamma?"

"You're awake," Isabel said.

"Gamma's house?"

"Gamma and Gampa," Ben said.

"And Norman?" Tony had fallen for Amelia and George's rowdy border collie. Amelia always welcomed his unending enthusiasm for helping her walk Norman.

"I'll come get our stuff later," Ben said.

"Okay." At first, they'd stayed at a hotel during visits, but a couple of months ago, Amelia had suggested they belonged at home, in Isabel's childhood room. Amelia wanted to see more of her grandson on their weekends in Pennsylvania.

"There's your mom."

Isabel shaded her eyes. October's sun made the snows of January seem like long-ago dreams. Her mom's plants seemed to riot in a last gasp of color and intoxicating smells over the wooden rails. Amelia waved.

"She's smiling," Isabel said.

Ben took Tony's hand and led him around the car. "Let's go see what that's about."

"Less go, Gamma!" Tony bolted up the walkway and Amelia caught him, falling against the door.

"You've grown, buddy." Everyone called him by Ben's pet name now. "Isabel, what are you feeding this boy?"

"Iz-bell cooks good chicken."

"And when did we master sentences?" Amelia beamed at Isabel, raising her cheek for a kiss. "He's like a weed."

"A busy weed." Ben smoothed Tony's hair. "How are you and George?"

"George is out back, fighting with the barbecue. Why that man won't switch from charcoal to gas…" Amelia led them into the living room, a dark-floored expanse of cool shade that featured plush plaid sofas and a condensation-laden pitcher of freshly squeezed lemonade. "Thirsty?"

"You bet." Isabel poured some into a toddler's cup Amelia had set out for Tony. She put the lid on and handed it to him and then poured three more glasses. "I'll wait for Dad to come in before I pour his."

"Here I am." Her father looked like his old self, smiling. He kissed Isabel's temple, something he did these days only when she left.

"Hey, Dad." Isabel shared a curious glance with Ben. Something had changed here. They usually saw her father after he'd run out of all the tasks he could set himself in the yard.

"Cookies, Tony?" her mom asked, holding up a plate.

"Cookies." He sang the word.

"What's up?" Isabel no longer avoided any uncomfortable conversation. "You two act as if you like us again."

"Give us a chance," her mom said. She mustered a smile that ended on a note of honesty. "Your father and I haven't behaved particularly well."

"We honestly thought you stuck together to keep Tony," her dad said. Her mom nearly excised him from the room with a sharp look. He jumped. "I'm not telling any lies, ever again."

"Sometimes tact is a choice, too." Isabel's mom reached beneath the table and came up with a bottle of champagne. "This is for you two."

"Why?" Ben dropped his hands on Isabel's shoulders. She sort of liked being protected when Ben was behind her.

"We know you want to get married," her mother said.

"But we figure you've been holding off because of us." Her dad flourished a hand at his living room. "What do you think of the fireplace as an altar?"

"Mom, Dad." Isabel blushed so hard she expected to see flames. "You can't—"

"We'll take it," Ben said, cutting in.

Isabel turned to him just in time to see Tony tap his dad's leg with a cookie.

"Want one?" he asked.

"No thanks, buddy." Ben patted his son's cheek, but he held Isabel with an intense look of love. "I'd like a wife."

The only sound in the room was Tony, chewing. He crunched an almond. "Mmm, Gamma," he said, as Isabel stared at Ben, fighting last-minute fear that her father's guess about their relationship was right. "Want more cookie?" Tony asked.

"I have some in the kitchen." Gamma took Tony's hand and then came back for Isabel's father when he didn't move. "Help me find cookies, George."

"I want to hear," he said.

"Me, too," said Ben.

"Dad, can we have a second?"

"I told you, George."

Even after they were gone, Isabel didn't know how to answer Ben's proposal. "Did you ask because—"

"Yes or no," he said. "I promise I'll never ask you to prove anything again, but I need to know if you'll marry me. We can talk about reasons later."

"Would you love me if we didn't have Tony?" she asked.

"You're cheating." He helped her up and traced the curve of her cheek with his fingers. After six months, he still looked at her as if he didn't believe she was his. She kissed his palm again and wished they could go to the little room under the eaves upstairs. It was easier to commit with her body than with words.

"I love you, Isabel, because you're as much a part of me as my arm or leg—or even Tony. We're indispensable to each other, the three of us, bound for life. I'll wait as long as it takes for you to believe in marriage again, but I need to know today if you will marry me. Sometime."

Isabel closed her eyes and saw Will that day she'd left—his relief that she was going. She could let him ruin her life, or she could choose to trust Ben. If he was willing to wait, she was willing to cut the wait short.

"Maybe the law requires a ceremony, but you and I have been man and wife for a while."

"What about those promises you needed before?" He nibbled the corner of her lips. "I'm dying to make them."

"You—sharing Tony with me—coming home to me each day with milk or a newspaper, or some other small thing we need. You—turning to me at night in that brand-new bed we bought—those are promises I believe in."

"Those aren't promises. You're talking about everyday life."

She wrapped her arms around him, knowing he was hers and she was his, and all was right. "Life in a house and a family filled with love."

HARLEQUIN *Super*ROMANCE

Big Girls Don't Cry

by
Brenda Novak

**Harlequin Superromance #1296
On sale September 2005**

Critically acclaimed novelist
Brenda Novak brings you another
memorable and emotionally engaging
story. Come home to Dundee, Idaho—
or come and visit, if you haven't
been there before!

**On sale in September
wherever Harlequin books are sold.**

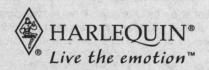

HARLEQUIN®
Live the emotion™

If you enjoyed what you just read,
then we've got an offer you can't resist!

Take 2 bestselling love stories FREE!

Plus get a FREE surprise gift!

HARLEQUIN *Super*ROMANCE®

is pleased to present a new series by
Darlene Graham

The Baby Diaries
**You never know where
a new life will lead you.**

Born Under The Lone Star
Harlequin Superromance #1299
On sale September 2005

Markie McBride has kept her secret for eighteen years.
But now she has to tell Justin Kilgore, her first love,
the truth. Because their son is returning to Five Points,
Texas—and he's in danger.

Lone Star Rising
Harlequin Superromance #1322
Coming in January 2006

Robbie McBride Tellchick had three growing boys and
a child on the way when her husband died in a fire. No
one knows how she's going to get along now—except
Zack Trueblood, who has secretly vowed to protect the
woman he's always loved.

And watch for the exciting conclusion,
available from Harlequin Signature Saga, July 2006.
Available wherever Harlequin books are sold.

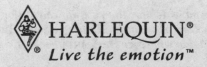